TALES FROM THE COLDBEANS GAZETTE

F Noel Graham

iUniverse, Inc.
New York   Bloomington

Tales from the Coldbeans Gazette

This is a work of fiction. All of the characters, names, incidents, organizations, and dialogue in this novel are either the products of the author's imagination or are used fictitiously.

iUniverse books may be ordered through booksellers or by contacting:

iUniverse
1663 Liberty Drive
Bloomington, IN 47403
www.iuniverse.com
1-800-Authors (1-800-288-4677)

ISBN: 978-1-4502-2518-2 (pbk)
ISBN: 978-1-4502-2519-9 (ebk)

Printed in the United States of America

iUniverse rev. date: 5/06/2010

DEDICATION

The stories in these four books are dedicated to my three mothers.

The first was my real mother who died when I was 3 and I do not remember anything about her except she loved me. My second mother was really my Grandmother who was too old to take care of a wild young boy but did her best. My third mother was really my aunt. She and my Uncle raised me along with their young son and I am sure I was a chore to handle.

I am who I am today because of these three women. Francis Noel Graham

NOTES FROM THE AUTHOR

First, I want to say that all these stories were created by me while drunk so I am not liable for anything you read. Second, yes I have seen a doctor and he said that for a man I am considered sane. I asked for a second opinion, he said I was also ugly. These stories were written just for you to enjoy and any resemblance to anyone kin to you or anyone that you know is your problem. I wish to thank the spell check on my computer otherwise you would not be able to read what I wrote after it was writ. Read this book carefully since a movie will not be coming later on. Last but not least please let me thank my creditors who really appreciate you buying this book

A BIT ABOUT ME

My Boss has no idea what I do as long as the computer is working and it looks like I am working the computer. I knew I had an advantage when I first came to work here and the boss asked me to do some typing for him on HIS computer. My boss is the old fashioned kind of boss that is still trying to figure out how to sharpen a ball point pen. His idea of spell check is to get the word close to right and let the type setter worry about it. Of course in that environment I quickly rose to the top of the little office. My boss has the big office not because he is in charge but because he is 300 pounds overweight. In truth he is not that fat but every thing goes to his stomach and nothing to his brain.

I have made it almost 5 years here by keeping my eyes open and my mouth shut. If I did that at home I might sleep better but a habit is a habit and that is why sometimes there are knots on my head. I have a good wife, she likes the kids and I pretend that I like her. She puts up with me so we have a good basis for living without killing each other. When the second kid came along I knew she was going to tell me that we were getting married but not here, maybe in Georgia. I took a liking to Coldbeans the first time I was here and heard the words "this is where we will live". I did the right thing and said "yes Maam".

Coldbeans is a pretty good little town where most of the people are dumb and the rest are stupid. The stupid people are glad they are not dumb and the dumb people are happy they are not stupid. Frankly I can't find the difference between them. If you like stupid people then this is the place to live. I moved here cause my pa moved here when he left my mom but she moved here also and so we are a fairly stable family. Thank god that I finished school before moving here. Some of the teachers are dumber than the students. In Coldbeans the main reason for going to school is that the parents can not afford a baby sitter. Another small reason is it is the law.

Bye the time I was in the third grade I thought I was smart enough to quit school but I kept going cause we were too poor to afford a baby sitter. That made me the smartest kid in town and also one of the smartest residents in town. My daddy was proud of my schooling and told me that if I kept it up I might not ever go to jail (other than to visit someone).

HOW DID THE TOWN OF COLDBEANS GET ITS NAME?

How did Coldbeans get its name? This is a bit complicated to explain. First there was a small boarding house, a few of the people would eat there when their wives were mad at them or they did not like what was for supper. Most of the clientele were men and being as men did not cook and only women cooked what they wanted to cook you ate what was fixed and that is all. There were no special orders. A few of the customers were women but they were ugly and real men did not talk to them partly because they were ugly and the other part being that the men's wives would beat their brains in.

This diner was called Sherry's but after awhile it became known as "Coldbeans". This was not a slam on the menu but because the men were used to cold beans for supper. Y0u make what the customer likes best and leftovers were their first choice. Since the town did not have a name yet the town took on the Coldbeans name. Now remember that this was a long time ago. Of course, there were several other names that had been suggested by the men but such names as liquor crossing or beer belly were not acceptable to the women of the small community.

WHERE WE ARE

Ever wonder where Coldbeans is located? A lot of people do including some who live here. Most people find us by getting lost and driving until they find someone to ask for directions. Boy are they disappointed with the answers to their questions from residents of Coldbeans, SC. You won't find Coldbeans on the South Carolina maps. We just did not tell the state or the map people that we exist and we are happy with everyone not knowing. Being "on the map" is not always a good thing. Sometimes it is only the curious tourist, the salesperson, or maybe the law looking for someone and we can do without any of those types of people.

We got what we need here and the Grocery store has vegetables grown locally and we trust the delicious taste of fresh picked and hand inspected vegetables. The clothes that Hiram orders from catalogs that he keeps under the counter for the women. Most women just want to buy patterns and make their own. The men can find tools in the general store but usually they just borrow them from a neighbor. Neighbors here trust each other and are caring. After all, if you live next door to the other guy all your life, you usually are kin to him somewhere in the past. The general store has Gasoline for use; but we don't use it much. We know that it has been in the hand-operated pump for at least 7 years and gasoline don't get better with age. We only have one church, and it ain't half full on Sunday. If it was not for the women, it would not even need to open at all. After all this explaining I will tell you, the location of Coldbeans is a bit north (we hate using that word) of Tarboro SC off route 321. Now I bet you don't know anymore than when I started. Look it up, it is there but the Town of Coldbeans is not listed. I guess you just ain't read what I have been saying.

HOW TO GET HERE

If by accident you make the turn onto the road to Coldbeans and most people who visit here do so by accident or are out of gas then please stop and look around for a bit. At first it may not seem to be an interesting place to visit or to live but in truth, it is a very pleasant place to live. We have no stress, very little crime, and very friendly people (except to their married partner)

When you first come down the road and enter Coldbeans, you see the General Store on the left. It is the largest building in Coldbeans. Across the street is the Mayor's office and in the back of his place, the side door on the right is the sheriff's office. This serves two purposes. It allows the sheriff to be close to the mayor and the mayor to keep an eye on the sheriff. They are not what you might call close trusting friends. You see the mayor wants to stay mayor and the sheriff wants to be mayor also.

Next door is the barbershop called "Shake's". No one gets a haircut there before noon so as to allow Shakey to calm down from his nightly binge at the jug. That's the reason for the nickname. On the side next to the general store is the livery. Now most of you might not know what a livery is but it rents buggies and horses and repairs them both. It also has saddles, reins, harnesses, and everything you need for traveling modes that do not use gasoline. The only gas pump is at the general store. We sell more kerosene than gas. Although electricity has been here for years, some of us have not cottoned to paying for it and some feel it is witchcraft. We are slow to accepting new things here.

Come visit us here in the spring or summer and you will find baskets on the front porch of the general store with tomatoes, cucumbers, okra, corn, peas and beans in bushel baskets all for sale. Not everyone here grows the same thing so the trading of produce is also practical. You can also call it barter. Oh, yes there is a small white church, Baptist of course and everyone attends the church. (The ones that make their husband go that is) "What was good enough for my parents is good enough for me" is why we only have Baptist here. It is a pretty church painted white and a real bell in the steeple. The bell is rung for Sunday services and emergencies in the community. God loves everyone and is pleased to see you here if you would like to visit.

COLDBEANS, A WINDOW ON THE WORLD

On the surface, Coldbeans seems like a tiny hole into the past. There are not many small towns left that are untouched by the life styles of today. Coldbeans lies down a small two lane secondary highway. If you were not going there on purpose, you would probably pass right on by the sign and not even know that you had missed Coldbeans. We like it that way. We cling to the past because we like the life we have now and that does not mean that we don't have some modern conveniences. We do enjoy electricity and washing machines (those of us that can afford them) Of course some of our town's folks are not too keen on bathing.

We even have a few TV's and even though we don't have cable we are pretty lucky to get good reception on our sets. A very few of us even have computers and that might seem strange to you, The contradiction of modern apparatus in a rural life is strange but some of us have gone to the big city and got an education and then returned to the land of our birth to bring some new things into the lives of these rural ways. We don't want to change everything but we want some progress, if not for the adults then for the children who someday will fly away and have lives of their own. Thus, even as I sit here in front of my desk, I can reach out to the whole world. I have friends I have never met and some that I talk to every day via chat on the net. It is amazing that I can converse with people from all over the good old USA and Canada and Great Britain and Germany, Australia and Newfoundland. Anywhere someone speaks English we can interchange ideas.

Communications is the key to all things in this world. It helps us understand each others and interchange new ideas. It teaches us that the world is big and there is so much out there. Our minds want to grow and need knowledge to do that. This little window is our outlet to the world and all its wonders and varied people and life styles

COUNTRY LIVING IS DIFFERENT

Coldbeans is a small town. It has only one paved road and that comes off the main highway and goes thru town on down the road to Too-kee-Doo, a much more cosmopolitan community. What make Coldbeans nice are its undisturbed natural surroundings. For those of you not familiar with the south (and everyone SHOULD be) I shall attempt to describe this hidden and unchanged piece of lower Carolina.

Coldbeans is a town plunked down in a very rural surrounding. The founding fathers were wise and did not cut down the trees to build a town. The town was built around the natural beauty of the land. Areas of 400-year-old oaks, draped with the ever-present Spanish moss, hanging like an old man's beard abound everywhere. In the old days, this moss was gathered and sewn into mattress bags to make beds and also stuffed into chairs and sofas to make them comfortable. In the old days, everything had a purpose. Bamboo from down at the river was used for fishing poles and to make many useful items such as chicken coops and to prop up the beans and tomatoes growing in the fields. Fields were plowed with the terrain to prevent washing away the black topsoil.

Cedar trees were cut and split to make everlasting fence posts. During harvest, the unusable parts of the plants were placed in the chicken coop and the hog pen. The hogs loved the sweet potato vines. The chickens ran loose under the house and in the fields. They knew that when dark came, they had to come home to roost. The chickens also ate the bugs from the vegetable plants and the chickens tasted delicious which is why they are called range chicken. Of course it was a bit of a problem finding some of the eggs but most chickens developed habits and laid eggs in the same place each time. The dogs were for hunting squirrel, rabbits, raccoons, possum's and other game. The dogs seldom ran the chickens. After all, they had been raised with them all around.

Houses were built on stones so they would be above the ground; this kept water from coming into the house in heavy rains. Rain water was collected in wooden barrels for bathing. I would not trade life in the country for an apartment in the big city, no way!!

TOUR THE TOWN OF COLDBEANS.

Here is just a little tour of our town for those of you who have not visited our little slice of heaven. It is not hard to get here if the directional sign is still up on the highway. We took it down for the election to keep the political candidates out. So far it has worked. On the left as you come in to town is the general store with its gas pump (manually operated) It has not sold any gas in 4 years. The gas in the pump is older than many of our kids. Across the street is the sheriff's office and barbershop and upstairs over the barbershop is where the town doctor (the barber's brother) works. You don't hear much screaming from upstairs; most of it is downstairs and it is from Shakey nicking an ear or something like that.

Up the street is the women's beauty parlor. No man has ever set foot in that place. We don't even know why it is called a "beauty" parlor because they come out looking like when they went in. It is a total waste of money. We think it is like taking a bath on Friday night, and having to do it all over again on Saturday. From the parlor, the town kind of gets rural. Up the road on the right is Hiram's place. It is easy to tell.

He is the only one with a bathroom attached. His family has always been rich. Further up the road, if you run across some cows wandering around without a purpose that is Elmer's place. He don't fence in his cows. It makes sense cause if everyone else fences in THEIR cows then why should he? His cows can't get into their fields.

Across the road from Elmer is "Pork Chop" Ledbedder. He raises hogs and they love him almost as much as he loves them. Pork Chop says if he ever meets a girl as sweet as his hogs he might marry her. We hope she does not have a sense of smell. I hope you enjoyed the tour of our little town but if it is paved roads you want, you must continue on to Bullpucky Swamp. It is only 12 miles away but we don't trust those people. Some of them wear ties and most of them wear shoes, even in the summer. Weird group they are. Some of them even go to church every week.

Why the name Coldbeans? That is simple. Hot beans are a once in awhile thing but eating cold beans can happen anytime you want to put some in a bowl The name of the town is a lot like the name of the main street "watchit!" Well it is not called that now because not many horses or mules use it but back when they did watch t was a common phase. It did save a lot of shoes, boots, and the floors in the stores. Today the main street is called, "Only" street cause it is the only street that is paved. What else would you call it?

Now, don't get us wrong, we eat more than cold beans of course but at that time, they were more often served than any other food. It did not matter what kind of bean it was, the white bean, the navy bean and even the damn Yankee bean was called Coldbeans when they were eaten without heating and if you have to fire up a wood stove just cause you want a snack then cold beans were not bad. See, sometimes the simplest answer is the right one, un- like the guvmint way of explaining things.

WHERE TO EAT

If you are hungry and can't eat at home then the option is the Coldbeans Café. Our local medical care recommends it as a great place to eat and the Café recommends the local medical care as the best place to go after eating. These two businesses are not connected but the Clinic is highly recommended in the café menu. One hand shakes the other as some people say. The café does not make you sick on purpose to give business to the clinic but they seem to be a symbiotic twosome.

The town doctor and the town sheriff work together to make sure that nothing you eat at the café will kill you. The town doctor specializes in food poisoning and the sheriff gets a cut from anyone that goes to a "recommended" lawyer who will send him to the "recommended" clinic. Both the town layer and the town doctor gets free meals at the clinic but both men prefer a bag lunch made by the woman of the house. After all if the town doctor got sick and the town lawyer gets shot then who will arrest the person who shot him? Logic and quick decisions are required in law enforcement. If the sheriff catches the person who shot the lawyer then he will be arrested but that don't mean much since the jail cell door has been broke for over 3 months now.

I don't know why a stranger would be in our town and better yet why he ain't skedaddled out quickly. He just had to be a salesman. All of our residents with at least a half a mind know not to eat at the clinic when there is better food at the Coldbeans Café. Heck even the sheriff can give you better food than the clinic. The women at the Coldbeans café have right good food and it is only a bit more expensive. Their customers only get sick if they order the "yesterday" special to save a bit of money.

TOWN VOTES

Well it is Election Day and everyone voted. The lines were long at the polling place. It seems like they had a new idea about speeding up the voting process so we would not have to wait so long in line. Of course it did not work out at all. The line was long until Benjamin cleared most of the polling place out. He is known for passing gas in some of the most crowded places. Fortunately, some of us are used to him and we could move up and get through the polling place quickly. We know already that the sheriff got re-elected because he was serving white lighting right outside before you went in to vote. We hope that you voted at least once for the person of your own choice. Good luck for the man you selected. This will be a short edition, everyone have a happy day.

COLDBEANS BLACKSMITH

Yes the blacksmith still plies his trade here. People have to have horses and horses need horseshoes, plows need mending, and buggies need wheels so there is still a need for a blacksmith. As required, there is a spreading chestnut tree outside the blacksmith's shop and the blacksmith is spreading just a bit too. It is hot work in the summer and a beer is good but leads to an occasional accident so the water bucket is the drink of choice.

The blacksmith is single and considered by some to be a good catch. Sadly, few black women in town are about his age. Thus, the blacksmith is probably doomed to being single forever. Being the only blacksmith in the area, he is very popular and business is good. Most blacksmiths worth their salt are also part-time vets too. They shoe a horse or mule, help deliver a colt or mend a sprained leg. They can also tell you if the animal is sick and what medicine to make it better. There is more to being a good blacksmith than just having a strong right arm. He is a friend to the schoolchildren who would rather watch him than go to a movie. Sadly the profession is a lonely one. You are called out anytime of the day or night, and that does not make for a good home companion.

Thus, when the right woman comes along it is time to take action. Such luck is rare and might not happen again in his lifetime. It is true that Annabelle was not good looking, in fact she had a bit of a mule face. She loved animals and also as it turned out, she loved the blacksmith as well. It was a relationship meant to be. They were wed in the blacksmith shop and instead of bells we heard the clanging of hammers on the anvil ringing out and hay was thrown at the bride and groom as they departed. Now Coldbeans residents are not stupid, they did not want to lose their only blacksmith, so a grant of 10 acres and a small house was donated for the couple to live. After 35 years, the fate of the town and the blacksmith were one. He was happy and so were the town folks. Maybe some day in the near future, a new blacksmith will be born and continue the family tradition of serving the town of Coldbeans. Isn't it nice when things work out? That does not happen often but when it does, it is time to celebrate. Hats off to the new couple and their future!

CALEB'S SOAP

"Skunk" Caleb came into the general store today to buy his semi-annual bar of soap. That's right, ANNUAL. He does not use much soap, and only takes a bath when his dogs start staying away from him. We think our general store is the only place in the state that still stocks Octagon soap and other than lye it is the only soap that will work on Caleb. Skunk is not popular with the town folks here and no one has ever invited him to church. Skunk lives off of what he traps. He used to hunt, but for some reason the animals could tell when he is in the woods and avoid him kind of like we do.

Skunk had a wife once but she died. They buried her while still holding her nose. Skunk was not invited to the funeral. The poor fellow gets lonely but sometimes we envy him, he doesn't have anyone nagging him to shave, bathe or comb his hair. Skunk must really get lonely though; even his dogs won't play catch with him. Bye the way, that store bought soap is a semi-annual occasion, he does use lye soap sometimes because even he can't stand the smell all the time and the flies keep him awake at night. Now as you know lye soap will clean anything. It is made of very fine ashes lard and lye. This is boiled until it is well mixed and then it poured into pans and allowed to jell, it is then cut to size and it will take anything but sin off of anyone. If you ever used lye soap, it might be better to go dirty.

A TALE OF TWO CHURCHES

If you come to Coldbeans for a visit and you go down church road about 4 miles, you will find a strange sight. There are two churches sitting close together both of them Baptist. There is a very nice concrete and steel bridge crossing a small creek that connects both sides. Each one is so close to the other church that you could see it clearly. You may wonder why this is so since both churches are Baptist and the same preacher preaches at both churches. Well, now as I have told you that things don't change much around here. Way back a long time ago, longer than anyone alive can remember both churches were active. Some went to one and some went to the other one. This might seem a bit crazy to you city folks but there is a sane reason for this.

There is a creek that divides the two churches almost equal in distance. This was back in the days of the horse and buggy and even in bad weather you went to church. Nothing could keep you at home on Sunday. There was no football back then to watch on a TV. TV had not been invented yet. When it rained, the little creek became a torrent of water and you could not ford it. At that time it did not have a bridge just a shallow crossing. The local doctor tried to ford the stream during a rainstorm and lost his life, his buggy and two fine horses. A good horse is a bitter thing to lose.

The families on the north side of the creek went to the church of the north side and the people on the south side went to their own church. You may ask why not all go to the same church when the weather was nice? The answer is simple. By then, some families would only go to the north church because their parents went to the north church and they would not think of changing and vice-versa for the people on the other side. .In fact, in a distance of 7 miles, there are 5 Baptist churches, some white, some black, some drinkers and some not. Over time, one of the churches, (the south one), lost most of its families to old age and so had only 6 people attending church. The north one had 43 people going there. The preacher still was required to preach at both churches.

You may ask why not combine them? Well guess you have never lived in the south. Family ties are strong and going to the other church would be like being unfaithful to your own kin, dead or alive. Now these same people would get together and have a BBQ or a big drinking party or maybe even a barn raising or celebrate a birth, but go to that "other church" no way! At least they did not dance what with them being proper Baptists church goers you know. Many country people cannot adapt to city life and many city people could never adapt to county life. There is only one reason for that. People are strange.

COLDBEANS JAIL

The jail in Coldbeans is not very modern. It would embarrass the town of Mayberry RFD. This is a small town and we do not need a lot of jail, mostly it is used for playing cards. It only has one cell and that is just used on Friday nights and sometime on Saturday. Those that get in jail on Saturday are let out to go clean up and get to church on Sunday. Now a city slicker might laugh at our little jail, heck, even the lock on the cell door has not worked for almost two years now. We are gonna get it fixed one day when we get the money. There ain't no locksmith near by and they charge an arm and a leg for coming out this far. Some of you might be a thinking that how can you lock someone up when there is no lock on the door? It is simple, when the sheriff is there no one tries to escape and when he is gone he locks the outside door. Besides, the sheriff knows who he has in jail and if the idiot just walked out the only thing the sheriff would have to do is go to his house and haul him back.

Some of you may also ask why you need a sheriff if only for the weekend. The answer is simple. During the week the sheriff is busy bottling his moonshine and no one wants that to stop. The sheriff makes the best shine for miles around. Matter of fact if you do spend time in jail he might share a snort or two with you. Some try to get in jail just for the free meal and the white lightning. As for the eternal card game going on, it is only a dime limit and no one loses much because it is cash only, no credit. The women whose husbands are in jail (never a woman is arrested here) can visit and bring enough food for the sheriff and a bit for her husband, who is more afraid of her than the time in jail. Yeap life is uncomplicated here, and we like it that way.

THE FRONT PEW

This paper got a question in the mail about our little church. In it a lady from Louisiana wanted to know if you had to sit on the front row (or pew) in church if you have your snuffbox and or bacca can. The answer (for our church anyway) is NO. You see, we had trouble filling up the front pew of the church. Only when the service is slap full as at Christmas or Easter do we need more room anyway. We took out the front pew and now everyone is happy.

The main reason no one liked to sit on the front row is that you can't check out who is wearing what and sitting with whom. Also the preacher talks kind of loud and this keeps those on the front row awake. Now the main reason for going to church is to see who is there and what shape their husbands are in and what the heck everyone else is wearing. In other words it is like any other church anywhere in this country. We are thinking of charging extra for use of the back row. It is the most popular seat in the house. It is mostly full of men who don't want to sit with their wives but had to come to church to keep the peace. You can tell from the loudness of the men's voices while singing just how drunk they were the night before.

The most useless chore in the church is that of being a collection taker. There usually ain't enough to make the trip down the aisle worth it. Most prefer to give in a closed envelope or trade for some chickens or eggs or maybe a side of bacon. It must be hard on the IRS to figure out our way of tithing. Many only suffer thru the service so they can get to the food afterward. We have the best tasting fried chicken in town and the sweetest watermelons and the coldest ice cream. It feels more like heaven outside the church than inside.

COLDBEANS FIRST MAN IN SPACE

This town has the distinction of having its first man in space. NASA selected our own Nathan "Cornears" Birnbaum for a special mission. Our town knew that someday Nathan would make good. He graduated third in his class in High School (there were only five kids that year and two kids dropped out to get married) Nathan was a bit of a loner and that is why NASA picked him in the first place, well that and because the monkeys all declined to take the mission. Nathan did not make friends; he stank a bit and picked his nose (on a date no less). Nathan's special qualifications of living alone made him the perfect choice to man the Mir Space Station. You see it is empty right now. All the Russians are over at the American station playing strip poker.

Our radio station covered the rocket take off and all of us listened. We wanted it on TV but our station has the old cameras and they are too large to transport. The takeoff was beautiful and a bit noisy. Everyone expects a rocket to make noise, what we are talking about is Nathan's screaming. The rocket made orbit ok and Nathan and his little spaceship was on the way to Mir. Nathan had strict instructions to not touch anything and that caused a big problem. Nathan had to go to the bathroom and could not hold it. No one told him where it was. That space ship now cannot be recycled. Nathan made it to the Mir station and settled in for as long as he could hold out. All he had to do was call mission control once a day. After a couple of months, he ran out of quarters for the calls and was not heard from for 3 more months before NASA discovered he was not calling. Nathan began to suffer from the closure and decided to step outside for a breath of fresh air He quickly discovered that he should have worn his suit. The door locked its self and he exploded in the vacuum. Some in Coldbeaners swear they saw the whole thing and if you look real close, you can make out a ring around Mir.

THE LEDBETDERS

Many people have a pet (a cat, a dog or a bird) that is normal, but Ethel and Uriah Ledbetder were poor and (lucky for Uriah) they had no children. His wife was ugly as wading in the swamp and did not smell much better. Uriah was no great catch himself so they were lucky they had no offspring
.

Everyone finds a pet a comfort on lonely nights and so when the Ledbether's hog rejected the runt of the litter; Uriah's wife suggested they raise it. The intention was to get it up to being able to be a pig on it's own and put it in the pen. The pig had other ideas. In the country, you just let your dog or cat out at night to roam about looking to get in trouble. The pig, now called "ham hocks" or ham for short, had no intentions of being a hog or running around outside with the common farm animals. Sure, he would go out to potty and run right back into the house squealing for something to eat. It seems that "ham" never got enough to eat. He would go looking for acorns when Hiram was with him, but he would go nowhere near the hog pen. I guess he considered them hogs a "lower class" of animal than he was. Having a baby pig is fun, having a shoat is also fun but when the shoat gets to be a hog, then it is time for the hog to go where hogs are suppose to go, (the smokehouse)

Never name a farm animal. That gives it special status and makes it no longer potential food. Now, as you know, Uriah's house is small and there is barely room for him and his wife. Add a 400 lb hog to the scene and times get a bit testy. One of the bones of contention was the bed. Hogs are not supposed to sleep in a bed (especially one build for two). Another problem is like most country folks; they built their own bed. It was a rope and pole bed. Two poles, one down each side and rope wound across the two poles and a mattress lain on top. When the rope stretched, then they would tighten up the rope, leading to the old saying "sleeping tight". (This is true).

So far there was no problem but the mattress was a sack made from muslin, a thin material that is cheap to come by. It is stuffed with dried corn shucks or sometimes Spanish moss, but the moss quite often has chiggers so they don' really like to use that. The corn shucks are from when the corn is picked and so when dried, makes a nice bed stuffing and it is free, a very attractive idea to poor people.

One day the Ledbether's had to go to town. They hitched the wagon and took off, forgetting that the hog was still in the house. Ham Hocks got a bit hungry and the only thing in the house that smelled tasty was the bed. By the time that the Ledbethers got home, the hog was full and the bed mattress was gone and ham hocks snored very contented in the middle of the ropes where once laid a mattress. Now muslin is easy to come by and corn shucks are always in supply so the bed was repaired and all was well, at least for the Ledbethers. As for poor old Ham Hocks, he made the best sausage and hams and was the centerpiece of the smoke house and he fed the family that had raised him for many months.

BAPTISM

After every baptism, the wild life complains about a fish kill down the ways in the creek. Baptism is only twice a year because in the summer it is too hot and in the winter it is too cold, the weather that is, not the water. The water is cold or cool all year long. The people like being baptized and do it twice a year, not just once in a lifetime. I think it is the water that they like, not the ritual itself. About the only man in this town who has not been baptized is Caleb and since he doesn't have a woman, there is no one willing to try to get him to the creek. Well he does go once a year for his bath but that is private because no one will be within smelling distance of him at that time and for sure there is no one who wants to see him naked. Now don't think that water is Caleb's enemy, it is the soap that he hates and only lye soap will clean him and that burns a bit. He bathes as little as he can get away with. You see, Coldbeans is just a normal southern town, just like a lot of others.

TIMES CHANGE EVERYWHERE BUT HERE

It is said that you can't go home and this is true in some ways, you can't return to the home you left because things change while you are gone but in your own mind, they should remain the way you want to remember them Coldbeans is an exception to that rule just like it is to most normal things. Here in Coldbeans you can go back. The small town of Coldbeans does change but so slowly that it is not noticeable. The kids that you remember are now the men of the town but that is about all. The buildings are the same, unpainted and wooden structures that are well used but not improved. There is no new construction, just the same old country store, fire station, barbershop, sheriff's office in the rear and the doctor's office upstairs. The streets are still unpaved, except for the main street, which is now part of the state secondary road system.

The people may be a bit older but on some it is hard to tell how old is old? The trees seem to remain the same, maybe a bit taller and larger but you would have to look close to see that.

The roads to the farms are still dirt most of the time and muddy the rest of the time. It's the people that make or do not make a town change. The town does not change if the people do not change. There is no change here because the people are happy and if you are happy, why change?

Did you know that this small town in lower South Carolina has its own

Indians? Yeap, some of the Yamacaw tribe from Charleston and the Ogeechees from Savannah started living here. Indians have respect for the land. They work it but do not harm it. This is a lesson we all should learn. America changes too fast, we should learn from what we have before we go on to something new. It is only when we lose something that we miss it and then it is too late to enjoy it.

SOLUTION TO THE PROBLEM

From the author of the Coldbeans Gazette.

I keep waiting for the Coldbeans stories to run out but with the intelligence of the people that live in Coldbeans stupid might live forever. It has been good that great simple wisdom came from a town that is proud that their people there are stupid. In fact, they are not stupid, they are just ignorant. It does no good to try to impart learning in a head that can not even remember what happened 2 minutes ago.

As I have said before stupid people seldom steal. They are not smart enough to steal (successfully). That is why I have always said that a resident of Coldbeans would make a good politician. That is only if you want an honest politician. If you want the professional crooks that work in Washington DC then don't try to change them. Right now in this country we are in a "mell of a hess" as my grandmother used to say. Suddenly living in Coldbeans is better than being in debt in the big cities. People are like kids. They want to borrow and spend next weeks allowance now. Some people are so deep in debt that they might have to be dug up many times to make them pay for their debt. This does not include the guvmint. It was born in debt and thinks that is the normal state for the country.

If all of Washington moved to our little town we would all have to seek another place to live. Most of our men's pants have 4 pockets and even for a politician that is a lot of pockets to pick except for most of us we have very little money to put in those pockets. Moving never solves a problem. Finding out what is wrong and what it takes to make it right is the way to do things. The only way to solve that problem would be to

let all the prisoners out of jail so we could put the politicians in jail. We won't have to feed them. Let them steal from each other.
From the author of the Coldbeans Gazette

COLDBEANS SALOON RULES

There are a lot of reasons that Coldbeans is the ideal town to live in. If you move your family here then you might be one of the smartest families in the whole town. The fact that you did not have to move here counts as 3 minus points on intelligence. If you move here to hide from the law then you might already know some of our citizens. If you move here cause you are broke, out of work and have no skills then you might want to run for the mayor's job.

You can't just decide one day to move to Coldbeans. First off if you have kin here they you can leach off of them for awhile before you have to find a job. If your wife goes to work then that will give you time to look for a job and also get to know the residents of our town. If you by chance meet the mayor then shake his hand. No need to give him your name unless you are thinking of donating to his campaign for re-election. If you are a single male and have most of your teeth the other men might not like you but the women will.

We do have a few social rules to follow here.

Never date a woman older than your own mother.

Never turn down a free beer.

Never offer to buy a beer for a stranger who is already drunk

If you are married do not tell others. It is none of their business and they might be jealous of you.

Never offer to buy a round for the others at the bar if you are drunk. Some of the other people might drink two or three beers on your tab. The most important rule is never taking your wife to the saloon. A female cramps the conversation and takes the focus off beer drinking which is why you should be there alone.

TAWKING NORMAL

We kind of talk a bit different from Yankee's and a lot of other normal people. One country town might say the same thing but in a different way. Of course the schools try to help and make all kids speak "English" or "American". We do speak American but with a slight accent. Since the accent is normal to us, it is youse guys who tawk funny. The worse English talkers are the English people themselves. It is hard to believe that we came from England.

Of course it is not only England but other parts of America talk funny also. Yankees are hard to understand and so are Cubans and most of the world. Even England does not talk where we can understand them. If you want proof of that then the next time you visit Coldbeans just listen to the way we talk. We are normal and it is YOUSE that sound weird. Thank God we never got the habit of driving on the wrong side of the road.

Yankees come down and want to buy some of our tomatoes. To us they are MATERS and not TOEmatoes. I guess that youse guys even have trouble with Rutabagas. A rutabaga is not a hog running around pleading for food. We also grow "sweet tattoes" and not YAMS! This country was settled by the English but we kind of messed up the "English" language and now speak American. We like "collards" not collard greens. We drink a "coke" not a soft drink.

Youse Guys up nawth have just got to learn to talk right like we does. After reading all of this you will be graded on a score from 0 to 10 and no cheating. Taking off your shoes does not help on a spelling test.

TOWN MODERNIZES

The town of Coldbeans is making progress daily; we now have some of the conveniences that the big cities, like the people of four holes swamp down the road have. One of the gang went to visit his cousin in Sweden (which is in South Carolina, not Europe) and discovered that his cousin was well to do and had one of those gadgets that heat the water so you can take a bath. He thought it was such a good idea that he gave it a good look over and decided that heck he could make one of them for himself. He trotted home and built a hot water heater out of an old 55-gallon oil drum but in his haste he forgot some of the safe guards put in by them commercial people. As you can guess, the men of Coldbeans not being as particular about their hygiene hate taking a bath in cold water and all the trouble it takes to bring in wood and heat water on the stove is very tiresome. So the idea of turning on the tap and getting hot water seems good to them. Well, there are pros and cons about do it yourself hot water. It seems like it is a good idea to put on a safety valve to prevent overheated water from bursting a right good drum but Horace didn't think of that. Alas, Horace had to replace a good bit of his roof and redo the kitchen. He also had to visit the doctor for a few burns on his privates and not to mention that it scared hell out of the hogs and chickens hanging around the house. The church is still trying to get his wife to move back in and forgive him for what was an honest mistake.

The town figured that with all the traffic going through town now that we needed a new traffic light. We now have one at the busiest intersection but it is tiresome to keep getting out the ladder and relighting the candle inside. I guess one day we will have to run some electricity up to the light. May all our readers have a happy thanksgiving and have lots to give thanks like we do for what we have here and are glad we live here.

A PERFECT EVENING

It is a warm night, one with a full moon and a clear sky. The air is a bit humid but pleasant when sitting on the front porch. We love sitting in the swing and having our arm around the one we love. Could life be more perfect? People of today don't know the pleasure of a front porch. In fact most homes built today don't even have a porch. They just have a small stoop with no place to place a chair or swing. Porches are great on mild summer evenings. Out here in the country, a porch is a simple overhang with wooden planks for flooring and a railing so you don't fall into the bushes after a few beers. Most people have an old couch so they can sit on the porch and also maybe a rocking chair or two. We have an old coke machine, the kind that holds coke bottles and crushed ice to keep them cold, except these machines hold more beer than cokes.

On a mild night, you can sit quietly and hear the crickets chirping and maybe a moth attracted to the light on the porch. Bout the only thing wrong is the mosquitoes biting. Off in the distance if you listen carefully you can hear the mournful cry of a train on its way somewhere unknown to us. The dogs play in the dark, chasing some critter that only they can see. The moon shines silver on the Spanish moss hanging from the old oak in the yard. The kids' have a tire on a rope hanging from the oak. It is hardly swaying in the slight breeze. The air is clear, no smog, no smoke, and no automobile fumes. This is just as God intended for life to be. It is peaceful here with no radio and no TV, but there are some good neighbors for company and quiet talk. This is the time of the evening that the neighbors get together. It is a quiet time, a time for sharing of the events of the day and the hopes of tomorrow. This is the country. The country is a lot different from the city, that place of hustle and hurry. The city never sleeps, some one once said. Well the country does and it sleeps peaceful with no sirens, no horns, and no ambulances screaming in the night. It is a good life but not for everyone. Some may find it boring and too quiet. We find it just right.

COUNTRY ROADS

Driving on a freeway, you do not notice what is going on around you. You are just looking ahead to see how far you are from the car in front of you for safety reasons while trying to get from where you are to where you are going as fast as you can. Country roads are not designed as a straight route or for fast movement from one place to another. Each turn in a country road has a reason. It is to avoid the big tree, or to cross a small bridge, where down the stream it would take a longer bridge to cross.

Country roads have shade to prevent the sun from making the driver hot, or the horse if he is lucky to be riding one. Country roads are for ambling along. They are slow paced, without worry because you can't get lost, as there is only one road and it goes from where you were to where you want to be.

You are never alone on a country road. People working in the fields stop what they are doing and doff their hat to you as a way of greeting. You can stop at a small stream and have a drink of real water. There are no additives in it. If lost, there is always someone to give directions and an invite to stay for supper. There are no motels on a country road. The real country roads are not tarmac; they are dirt, with wheel ruts from travel by horses pulling loads to market and old pickups driven by old men on their way to try to sell some of their goods and wares. The air smells different also; it is clean, fresh and sweet, as nature should smell. It makes you wish that the trip did not have to end, but suddenly you came back to the real world, smelly, hot and busy. Country roads, take me home, to the place where I was born. Truer words were never said

FATTEST PERSON IN TOWN

Lucy was the fattest person on town, and she wanted to do something about it so she went on a diet and really stuck to it. In just three months she had lost over 17 pounds and was proud of herself. She would go look at the cakes in the general store and the candy counter and drool. This devotion helped her to lose. Admittedly it did nothing for her disposition but she was losing. When you are living with someone on a diet it is the worse thing that can happen outside of being captured by the enemy and tortured. Well maybe not...but they are equally painful. The sad thing is Lucy started looking good and the men noticed her. It is all women's dream to want to be desired by someone but the husband did not share it, so he ate to comfort himself and gained the weight that Lucy was losing.

Lucy got to thinking that she needed more changes that just losing weight. The more she lost, the prettier she got and the more depressed her husband got. Now some women like a big man. When he is around, the woman looks thinner and that helps their ego. Remember that Feminine logic is the world's greatest oxymoron. Lucy was looking good and wanted a new partner and all of a sudden, her husband found that some women did not mind a rotund man and thus he was desirable too. The scene was set for a divorce.

The divorce was quick, each happy to be free. Being single again changed their way of thinking about things for both of them. Lucy was now slim, single and happy but no man seemed to want to hook up with her in matrimony. Lucy's ex was also finding that being single was not all he thought it could be. Women love to entice a married man, but once single, the excitement was gone from the contest. Lucy, now being single, slim and available, and her ex being fat single and available found they were more lonely that when they were a married couple. Lucy began to eat and gained back her weight, meanwhile, her ex was despondent and lost his desire for food, and thus lost weight.

Lucy and her ex decided it was time to talk so they set a time and had lunch together, the talk turned into a date, and both of them had fun just as they used to do in the old days. They found that it was not the weight that caused the problem; it was the lack of excitement in the marriage. Both are happy now, and Lucy has kept off her weight and her ex has lost some also and they make a happy couple and there is joy in Coldbeans again. There was only one sour note, now that Lucy was thin, she was no longer the fattest woman in town, and the new holder of the title was very mad with Lucy.

COLDBEANS OLYMPICS

We here in Coldbeans, being a small town decided to not send someone to the Olympics. We do have our own contest of physical skills, some of which you might not find in most athletic events. We have the watermelon spitting for distance, which seems common in a lot of areas but we add a little difficulty to the event by making the contestant chew tobacco before spitting the watermelon seed. The viewing audience stands way down range from the landing site for this event. Another game, which we borrowed from our neighbor in Georgia, is the diving belly flop into a muddy puddle. This one is best viewed from a safe distance also. Contestants are judged as to their creative skills on the leap into the mud, points for belly flops and more for flips and extra points if you get mud on a spectator.

The greased pig contest is not the ordinary one that most people think of. Here we use one of Clem's boys. He gets all greased up and to add to the difficulty Clem's boy does not take a bath for two weeks before the event. He is also encouraged to eat lots of boiled eggs before the contest. This test of skill is best watched from upwind if possible. We also make a little money on the "kiss the pig booth". Ms. Martha is in charge of picking the ugliest girl in town to be the pig in the booth. Some girls take it as an honor and some do it just so they can be kissed. You lose points if you hold your nose or close your eyes while kissing her.

This Olympic contest is so popular that it sometimes brings the politicians from Columbia to watch which adds to the smell around Coldbeans. We considered cooking chitlins to raise funds for the kids but the smell of the politicians was so bad that the people could not eat the chitlins.

SIGN PAINTERS

Part of my early life was spent as a sign painter apprentice I worked for a very patient and kind man named Claude and this was to be my chosen profession for a while. Now in some areas, sign painters do not share a very good reputation. They are fly by night so you never pay before the job is done and approved. Never loan them a few bucks or your sign might just be part done and the painter long gone. Sign painters do not work all the time, only when they are broke and need money for booze. Yes, booze, any kind, beer, whiskey, paint thinner etc. Be clear what you want on your sign, the colors and where you want it painted. Jobs have been known to be completed and a fine job too but on the wrong building or the wrong side of the right building. Also make sure you check the spelling of the job with the painter before, during and especially after the job.

Not all sign painters are alkies and vagrants; some of them are very talented. This malady passes over from house painters and some other profession also. Thank god, we have only one sign on one building, and sure enough it is not on the correct side, being as it on the rear of the store makes it hard to read unless you go out back. When driving thru the country, look for the barns with the sides all painted with signs. It is a ollectable photo as that art is disappearing. So far, only one not to bright woman in town has been talked into having a Tobacco ad painted on her house. She thinks it is pretty, but then she also thinks her husband is handsome and that all the other women want him.

NOT ALL HERE ARE CLODHOPPERS

Not all people here in Coldbeans are stupid clodhoppers. There are some clever and smart men here. Now clever means the ability to know when to talk and when to shut up and what to do with what you learned. Smart means knowing how to get out of trouble without getting into more trouble by trying to get out of trouble. Most of the men who fit this description are politicians, local, and county, but this story is about WOMAN, Gods greatest gift to man. Now to man women are the very essence of his troubles and because of her he must take a bath and shave and come home sober and work daily. Real men put up with that for a good woman. Men are always trying to prove that they are right but never seem to win when arguing with their woman.

This is about none of the above. This is about the real woman, the kind that every man desires and few have and those that do know how lucky they are. A good woman is beautiful, not in the physical way but in the eyes of her lover and children. She is the gracious queen in the living room entertaining guest, a gourmet in the kitchen dazzling the palette and a whore in the bedroom, in private and with the lights off. A real man, should he be lucky enough to have such a woman and guard her all the time. He is aware of the treasure he has and that no amount of money could replace her. She is loved because of what she is and is adored because she returns the love. To view her creates a yearning that does not diminish with time but only increases in intensity. No matter how young she is or how old she is, she is beautiful, and only becomes more beautiful with time. Her charm is a rare gem, more precious than gold or diamonds and cannot be created or bought.

Her soul is free and in her freedom, she binds herself in love for eternity to that special person. Such a woman does exist, sometimes she is there but hidden because of blind male eyes that cannot see the great beauty he has. Her beauty will only shine in the reflection of her lover's eyes and will be a light eternal. She is rare and so should be protected and worshiped. Does this woman exist in your life? Are you sure? Look deeply and see the reflection of your love for her. Protect this woman. Her love is free to the man who has her heart and she will be faithful to his adoration. Woman is to man just as the rainbow is a promise from God. Be thankful we for once in our life get to enjoy such a treasure.

WHERE IS THE MONEY

What is wrong with this picture? As an American my money goes to taxes for many things and part of which is education. Now my money goes to Washington so they can send part of it back to my local county to build schools and hire teachers? Why not cut out the intermediary and keep the money HERE! Every time money changes hands, the amount gets smaller. The Guvmint gives us nothing. The money they send to us comes from our pockets and when it is returned, it is always less than what we sent to Washington. Why do we need a "bored" of Education in Washington? All we need is a small office to make sure that all of the states are doing the same thing. The more offices in Washington the more of our money is spent and not spent well, I have to say. Our Guvmint as with all guvmint's does not generate any income; they only have your money to spend, and none from their own pockets. Ok we have to pay them so why can't we ask for better results for our money? Don't complain about "big" business, complain about "big guvmint"

THE LOTTERY WINNER

Grace, aunt Tilde's daughter, just won the SC lottery. Well not the big money but 1500 bucks, which for down here is a whole passel of money. She is thinking of enlarging the house with the money. Right now that would be a good idea because two of her daughters are pregnant again and they sure could use the additional rooms. It is amazing that when you really need something, fate steps in and helps... Grace really needed a car but she can't spend the money twice, only our guvmint can do that. Grace has just got to get a hand on those two daughters of hers. They have most of the boys in this town scared sick that they are the fathers of the "mishap"

The church here frowns on single mothers but most of the girls want to try motherhood before getting hitched and then find out that marriage was not for them. It seems that being a single mother is better than being a divorced woman. Being a good mother has nothing to do with being a wife. The two are not mutually connected. There is a lot of fighting and fussing in a bad marriage but a lot of loving in a family

WHERE IS THE TOWN?

When you drive thru Coldbeans, you do not see many buildings other then in the main town. Pasture or fruit trees out on the farms hide most of the buildings. Only a small dirt road may tell you that someone lives there. There is not even a mailbox. We don't have mail delivery here yet. Many of the buildings in the main part of town are combined for the convenience of the customers. The barbershop and the hospital are very close to each other for reasons well known. Shakey is the barber and the hospital gets most of his business since his brother retired.

The Sheriff's office is right behind the general store and there is a reason for that too. The back of the general store is where liquor is dispensed (the legal stuff that is) this makes it easy for the sheriff to see what is going on over there. There is a drive up window with a blind Marie drawer. What! You don't know what a blind Marie is? Well you see, most people here like to drink but the Baptist are not supposed to drink so how do they get the legal stuff? They get it through the blind Marie drawer of course. You drive up and put your money and a note of what you want in the drawer and the owner then sends you back your bottle and change. This way no one can see who is buying the devil's brew and their privacy is protected.

It is rumored that soon the Baptist will be able to drink out in the open and they will be able then to shake hands in the Liquor store or as we call them here "doctor red dot," because of the SC law that says all liquor stores can not have a sign but must display a red dot on the outside wall. This goes back to the days before most people could read. Anyway, it works real well around here. It keeps you from being embarrassed when you meet one of the deacons from the church in the store.

GOOD OLD OUT HOUSES

One of the things that you would not like that we had to contend with was where to put the toilet. For emergency nighttime use and on cold night we kept a "slop jar" under the bed or somewhere near by. Having to put on clothes and shoes to run to that little house with the half moon in the dead of winter was not something we liked. The slop jar was not a healthy thing but was useful. The outhouse was a better deal but was not heated so was not comfortable and you could not read if you went during the dead of the night. The best way was to train yourself to wait till daylight (if you could). Now it does get cold here in the winter. It also gets powerfully hot here in the summer and that was the other problem. At least on a cold night, the smell was not too bad. Some people got the bright idea of a trap door in the roof that would open and let out the bad air and let in some light. This was not useful on a rainy day (or night) the old joke about the sears catalog was true but other methods worked also. Corncobs were plentiful and worked but were painful. No one said that the "good ole times" were always fun. That was just the way of life at that time and we did not know of the things that are now taken for granted in this age.

GIVE TO OUR FUTURE

We do not want our children to grow up and be president some day, but if that did happen we hope that he would be a good president and when he leaves office the country a bit better off.

We raise our kids to a standard that we want to feel is what we ourselves would do. We try to give them the best we can within the limits of what we have to give. If we succeed only a little bit, we have added to the good of the entire community and the country and the world. Maybe that small success will multiply with the future generations and this will someday be a better world, in part for the tiny bit we put into raising our children and what the rest of the country put into raising their children.

There are no millionaires here, we are all dirt poor but we have a pride in self and a pride in country. We worry about wasting our vital resources, oil, coal, forest etc. The most valuable resource is our CHILDREN. Make America better by giving America better adults to mange this country. That is the mission of parents and I believe that it is in the hearts of all parents.

TV ADS DON'T WORK

A few of the richer people here in Coldbeans have gone and bought themselves a TV. Not the big old monster TV's that you see in the big city but small black and white jobs that sit on the stand in the living room and the whole family can see if they sit real close. The only problem with TV is that some ignorant people are taken in by the ads on TV and buy the stupid stuff that they tell you to buy. Take Clem for example, he saw this ad for Epplystop hair remover (not the real name, law suits you know). It said it would remove hair and even came with a nice robe. Clem got the hair-brained idea (no pun intended) that this stuff would be good at hog slaughter time. Cleaning the hair off a hog is time consuming and not fun. Clem figured that if he used this stuff on the hog and it worked, it would be worth the money and the ad said a lifetime supply. Well it did and did not work. It seems like some of the hair was removed or in truth fell off the hog and the hog took sick. Clem had used the whole bottle on one hog.

This was going to cost more than he wanted to pay. Clem went back to doing the hog killing the old fashion way and his wife was happy with the robe until she tried to wash it and the fuzz fell off the robe and into the tub. Clem did manage to make some good of the product though; his wife looks a lot better without her mustache and goatee. Do not believe everything you see on TV, specially the news and politics. Nuff said!!!

COLDBEANS TEST FOR NEW RESIDENTS

The following test is for people that think they would like to live in Coldbeans.

#1 How often do you take a bath?

Daily
Weekly
In the summer
Annually

#2. How do you tell when your wife has left you?

It is quiet around the house
You start to get hungry
You find yourself watching a lot of football
You get a letter from a divorce lawyer

#3. How do you know when you need a bath?

You think there is something dead in the fridge
The wild animals stop coming around
The mail carrier leaves a note that he can't come around anymore till you bathe

#4. How do you know when it is time to leave Coldbeans?

You start wanting to find a job.
You get lonely
You wish you had your wife back
You find yourself answering yourself when you talk
If you found this test too easy and did not need help with it.
If you found there were questions that you could not answer
If you could complete the test without an adults help. Coldbeans is not for everyone but we like it here.

GOLDIE GOES TO THE MOVIES

This is a true story but the names and location has been changed to protect the editor from lawsuits. Our little town has no theater so when we want to see a show we must go to some other place, Too kee do has a nice but small theater. There is only one problem with it. The owner treats it as her private place and sets the rules and the kids that go there do not like to be controlled.. A dear friend celebrated Mothers day with her two sons by allowing them to take her to the movies to see Spiderman. Now one thing you must know is that Mary (not her real name) is blind and has been for many years. She has adjusted to life and now enjoys doing whatever her sons wish and it was their wish to treat her to the theater.

Mary was accompanied by her working dog (Seeing Eye) it is also her full time companion and they go many places together. The evening started wrong with the asst manager of the restaurant they picked. First being unaware of the special status of working dogs, he denied them access to the restaurant if they insisted on bringing the dog in. After much debate and the manger showing up, the assistant was greatly admonished and Mary and her two sons got free meals.

Then they went to the theater where there was no problem getting into the show but the person inside did not want to let the dog in and could not understand why a dog would want to "see" the movie. One of Mary's sons told the man that his mother only listened to the show but the dog was the one that wanted to come see Spiderman. That bon-whit cracked up the man and so "Goldie" the working dog, had her own seat in the theater and enjoyed the movie as well as the humans did. Some times humor is best found in real life, one must just be looking in the right way for it.

COLDBEANS CELL PHONE

We have had a few inquires as to our reference of the food "chitlins". They are hog intestines, cleaned and washed several times, battered and deep-fried. They are delicious according to those who have eaten them and lived. We are progressing into the 20th century, I know it is the 21st century but give us time as we are slowly catching up. We now have one color TV and when we get an antenna for it, it should be fun to watch. We have several black and white TVs and a few phones in the home (most of them coin operated). The town now even has a cell phone.

The cell phone belongs to "honest Abe" Hornsby, a local car and buggy salesman who kind of got caught being a little less than "honest." He is doing 6 months in the city jail and that is where he has his "cell" phone. It is a pay phone in his cell. He is still very much in contact with all his interests. It seems that not everyone trusts those who work for "honest Abe"; His employees are costing him a bunch of dimes daily.

Of course this does not make the sheriff happy. The jail is normally empty during the week and the sheriff can then brew his evil hooch but not with "honest Abe" watching.

"Shaky" the barber has hired a shoeshine boy but the kid is not making any money. Most around here wear plowing shoes or no shoes at all and the women don't haunt Shaky's place. The kid is enterprising though; he is painting toenails of those who go barefooted and washing feet for $1.00 per foot. He ain't doing bad at it as long as he holds his nose while working.

MELON HAID, OUR GENIUS

We un's here in Coldbeans got us a genius, even though he is only in the 9th grade. Being in the 9th grade is praise enough since no one else has made it that far. His teacher is beaming with pride. Now besides being smart, Melon head as he is known (his real name being Mel Haide) also is a free thinker. He don't need being taught stuff like the rest of us. Melon might someday be a scientist with the way he is going. The scientific mind in him makes him the free thinker he is. He lives outside the normal way of thinking that we use. He thinks about things other than girls, food and smoking rabbit baccy.

Just the other day, he amazed the whole class (which, by the way ain't too hard to do) with his revelation that being that oil is lighter than water so when an oil tanker is full it sits further out of the water than when it is empty. Now he is trying to figure a way to add more oil to the ship and then it won't even touch the water. Can you tell me that you could have thought of that?

Course now, like most "genius" he ain't too bright in social ways. He is good looking and got three girls in a family way, two of them he never slept with. This illustrates that genius and stupid are two sides of the same coin. I might be able to find Melon a job with the paper, but since I can only afford one lazy worker (and me) I will have to fire Ronald again. Oh well. I enjoy firing him anyway.

OUR RIGHT TO BE WRONG

Here in Coldbeans we only have one place of worship, a small Baptist Church that everyone attends, especially on the Sundays that we have an after church social. We were surprised to see that the judges of the Supreme Court in their wisdom have banned prayer at football games and other sports and even at graduations and most common gatherings. What happened to God in America, has he gone out of style?? Now we would expect that in Russia or some other communist country, but not America! Why just look at our coins, "in God we trust" which really means we cant' trust anyone else BUT God. Of course, here in Coldbeans, we do not have enough kids smart enough for football or baseball but if we did, I bet they would pray before a game.

The House and Senate in Washington start each day with a prayer with their paid chaplain. The president is a perfect example of paying lip service to religion without obeying its teachings. I don't know if the Supreme Court has any prayers in their big place of business but I bet they need it. Why is this country that was build on religious freedom gone away from God, the answer is simple, it is spelled ACLU. They are here to protect us from things that they feel we are not smart enough to protect ourselves from.

Now take our little Baptist church, The Baptist feel that we should not have 'petticoat" preachers (that means a female pastor) and lots of people feel that is wrong. But not us! We like Gloria; she is just what we need and want. Being Baptist we could boot her anytime and get a man but we don't want to do that. What is wrong with a woman being a church leader in this new millennium? Are not women as smart as men? It is the women who run most of the houses here and set the rules for the family. This country in its desire to protect its people from harm is doing more harm than good. Let the people in their own wisdom decide on their own what is wrong. Sometimes we will be wrong but it is our right to be wrong at times.

RAISING KIDS

Raising kids is not the hardest task in the world, world peace is but raising kids is I do not doubt maybe the second hardest task. Kids have a natural born curiosity that is equal to their intelligence. When a child is born their entire world is new to them. They learn from the first moments. They soon know their mothers voice and soon how to reach out to her and to hold. They explore and in doing so, they get hurt. Let a bee sting just once and the lesson is learned to stay away from bees. Skin a knee, get hit by a ball, fall down; all these things are learning lessons. Here in Coldbeans we have kids with rifles, some under the age of ten, but they have been carefully taught the dangers and rules and most of all, the big rule, disobey and loose the right to carry the rifle. This threat will make a boy think before he does some silly thing as shooting at a poor bird for fun.

The world is dangerous, but here in Coldbeans, it is not quite so dangerous because we teach our kids Respect, right from wrong and most important, what will happen if you do not obey the rules. That is a practice that the big city could use. The back woods and rural areas are safer than the inner cities of this country and it is because of the parents here that have made it so.

GOOD NEIGHBORS

Keeping in touch and never a lender or borrower be is ok for city folks but here it is a necessary and a natural part of life. Borrowing is necessary, we don't have all the things we need such as a bottom plow, or a large wash tub and who wants to spend good money on something that is seldom used? Someone in the neighborhood will have what you need, no matter what it is. All you have to do is ask someone and they can tell you where to go to get it. That is just being neighborly and the other important part is returning the item when through with it, clean and in the same shape as when you got it.

This works for everything but children, no one borrows kids unless it is to help with a chore and then kids are rewarded with something nice, not money, but maybe some cake or ice cream. That big insurance company ain't the only good neighbor! No neighbor will turn down the asking of a favor unless they don't have that item or the time to do the chore that you ask. Even then, they will volunteer the name of someone who can help you with that problem. This makes for good neighbors but does not help the poor guy down at the general store. Being a good neighbor is making him very poor, but after all, he too borrows from his neighbors.

IRAQ SOLUTION

You know what we need in Iraq. We need more Female soldiers and a few female generals too. Nothing will piss off the Iraqis terrorist more then to get whooped by their "inferior" enemy. Hell has no fury like a woman scored. Send a squad of "Hillarie's armed guard who are in the middle of their menstrual period; to fight ands see the enemy run. I wish l we could do that but I bet there is something in the Geneva Convention like an article about cruel and inhuman warriors (which is a great oxymoron) Oh well, it was a good idea.

JASBO AND LALUE

Jasbo was dying and he knew it so he put an ad in this paper saying that he was dying and had no one to leave his money too. He got a lot of offers but here in Coldbeans, the pickings for a woman ain't so good. Most are ugly as a mud fence and the ones that aren't as ugly as a bucket of homemade sin are mean as a twice run over snake. Only problem with all of this is that Jasbo did not die, well not right away, in fact it was almost 21 more years until he died. Now that puts a hardship on a woman who got married for money and had to keep the husband till death to get that money. The wife (named Lalue) had a bunch of men waiting for her to be a widow so they could marry and get some of that money and besides with money Lalue became a lot more attractive.

Well, as it turned out, Jasbo and Lalue after a bit of time really fell in love for true and not for money. Yes true love. Jasbo got so well that there were two kids born, and the kids were healthy and fine. Now a happier couple you could not find anywhere. 15 years of marriage and it ended, unexpected. Lalue died. After the funeral and the proper time the women started to come a courting. Some were nice looking by Coldbeans standards, (that meant they had most of their teeth) Jasbo never did marry again and his lovely little daughters grew up and were the catch of the town but some dang Yankee from New York beat out the whole gang of our boys

The younger daughter was happy living in Coldbeans. She got married and made some boy miserable for years. The other daughter and her wonderful husband are now the parents of two kids, and guess what; they want to move to Coldbeans to be where their grandpa lived. If you love someone, let them go and if they love you, they will return.

JIGSAW PUZZLES

Before TV for entertainment you could listen to the radio. It had good stories like Boston Blackie, Mr. Keen, tracer of lost persons and all the soaps and a bit of news. The nice thing about radio was you could work or be in the other room and listen while you were doing something else. The family sat around and listened to the radio. Parents in chairs, kids on the floor and they listened to the great cowboy series and good comedy with no fowl language. It was a family medium. We kids could play on the floor with our toy soldiers and jacks.

Another great past time, one that is still here but lacks the wonder of the old was doing jigsaw puzzles. They were not the over enhanced photographic puzzles of today but were some of the great works of art. Seeing some of those works is what gave me the desire to paint, and I love to paint even now. My grandmother had hundreds of them. Some were marked "one piece missing" some were such a tight fit that you could roll them up and put them back in the box. They could be taken out and worked over and over again and with a thousand pieces, you did not remember the assembly, and it was always the same pleasure as the first time that you did them.

With progress, if that is what it really is we have lost so many of the true pleasures of life and also lost our childhood. Believe me the future is not as good as the past was.

HOW TO RUN A SMALL TOWN

Coldbeans is preparing for its annual "watch Clem get a bath" celebration. This happens only once a year and is a big event around here. Before he would wash in private in the creek but now that he is married, Mrs. Clem does it to him. People start making lye soap months before the big event and everyone turns out to watch (from a distance of course). That is why Mrs. Clem is washing him. When he gets to stink too much for the house and it is springtime, everyone knows it is Clem washing time. Mrs. Clem went and bought an old claw foot bathtub and put it in the yard. They started cutting wood for the fire to heat the water (Clem does not like cold water). In fact he don't like any kind of water. Once he got out of the tub and took off to the woods with his wife and kids a chasing him. They caught him in a briar patch and boy he was glad to get back to that tub.

OUR HOPES ARE IN THE KIDS

Modestly I say that I am the smartest man in Coldbeans. This is not hard to say since most of the men here have trouble remembering which leg to put in which hole in his underwear. These people are not uneducated, they are just not bright. After all it has not been that long ago that they did not have a school for the kids and the only way we got a school was to tell the mothers that the kids would be away from the home for 5 hours a day (or when the teacher ran out of booze). We have tried out 7 teachers since Coldbeans got its own school house. 4 of them have recovered after distracting the husbands and the other three are in parts unknown to us.

Education is not everything. The ability to know right from wrong and when to go to the bathroom and when to keep your mouth shut when the wife is talking is the best survival technique used to avoid sudden headaches. The school does a great job with the kids and it is the adult males that we have trouble with. For many of our men learning is a bit too late for them. Besides if they were smarter they would run like hell from home and the wives do not want that to happen.

We want our kids to be smarter than we are but frankly I think that might be a pipe dream. You have to have some smart genes in at least one of the parents to hope for a brighter child.

VOTING TIME

We here at Coldbeans are pretty much laid back and don't let much of the real world bother us. That is why Coldbeans votes every election and every one votes. They may not all vote the same but they do vote cause it is one of the ways to let our opinions be known to those Washington people. Once every four years we have someone come around and promise us everything we want, then he leaves and we quickly forget what he said. It is the only way to run a country.

REDMAN'S REVENGE

All of you know of the tragic damage done to the Indian back in the old days. The white man in his arrogance thought that his way was the right way, the Indians were just heathens, and they tried to wipe the Indians out. Not all white men hated the Indians but those that did were far in the majority and in their time, they honestly thought they were right. Today, the trace of any Indian blood in a person is a reason to brag, the native man is seen in a better light, and his life style is now better understood. The cowboy movies did not help and neither did the legend of Gen Custer (who by the way was not a General at that time but a Lieutenant Colonel). All legends have a way of getting in the way of the truth. All this was said to make a point.

The noble red man did get his revenge and caused the death of more white men than any Indian war in history. How did he do it you ask? Simple! He had Sir Walter take a bit of tobacco back to the queen and it soon became the rage of nobility. It is still adored by those who use it and they do not know that they are hooked on the "Indian's curse". Put that in your pipe and smoke it, white man.

BROKEN AXE, SC

This story is not about Coldbeans but a story from the town of Broken Axe, SC There is a unique family there, the mother of the family had 8 girls. She just loved being PG and her husband, poor fellow, wanted a boy but never was that to happen. Thus, the town of Broken Axe was created and all from one family and one farm and named after an axe that was driven into a tree so hard the owner could not get it out. He broke off the handle and left it in the old oak.

The poor husband, his name forgotten, finally got fed up with a passel of women around and no boys to inherit his name so he up and ran off to parts unknown. All of the girls as they grew, developed the same craving for being pregnant and each of them when they reached the right age (14 in SC), the boys was willing to help them out. Each of the girls was successful many times and thus a very large farm with lots of houses. This farm or soon to be town was a great hang out place for the boys but none wanted to move there. The girls all gave birth to girls and all of them took the family name so as not to confuse each other with remembering so many new names.

There is no perfect place, even heaven had the devil until God booted him out and so too that is how it goes with Broken Axe. Whoops, a boy was born there! I don't know if it was heaven or hell to have so many women, all kin to wait on you, but this lad did and he had to wish for nothing. The uniqueness of this town was so intriguing that the University of Southern South Carolina even sent a team of two men to study this area. During their visit they got two of the girls pregnant and for some reason the study was incomplete and never recorded. Most of the girls, now about 37 of them, still live in the town (or farm) in peace with only one brother. Visit sometime but keep your pants on or you might some day have kin in Broken Axe.

HERO OF COLDBEANS

Coldbeans has its resident hero from the civil war or as we call it "the recent unpleasantness." In the front of our town hall stands the statue of Jebediah Lee. He saved Coldbeans single-handed and it was an accident. You see, Sherman was attacking us and we had our men hiding in the trees waiting for him. Jeb lee was the captain in charge of the unit and he saw that Sherman's troops were pretty strong and we didn't have a chance. So he whipped his horse to skedaddle out of there and the horse ran right toward Sherman's troops.

Our troops, seeing the captain whipping his horse and charging right into the thick of the battle, got inspired and got up and supported him in his brave action. Jeb was hit by a bullet in the arm and was decorated by General Thomas of SC. Later on he was elected Mayor of our little town, which was a lot smaller than it is now. Jeb skimmed a lot of money out of the town funds and even had enough to have a statute of him erected outside of the town hall where it still stands.

Of course, the statue does not look so much like Jeb since he skimmed on the funds for building the darn thing. It is cast out of concrete and even that was not right. It is cracking and falling apart, one arm has fallen off. (It was the one with the sword upright), and the head turns around with the wind. Somehow that part seems appropriate of the old coot. Jeb lost his next race to be mayor after the people found out what he had done, but the people thought maybe he should be in congress so they sent him to Columbia, our capital. JEB Lee never made it into the history books but we have a fondness for that crooked fellow, he was one of us.

AN OLD FASHIONED CHRISTMAS

Here in Coldbeans as usual, Christmas is different. Actually, it is not different because it is like the old days before K-mart and Wall-mart and credit cards. People do not run around looking for some store to buy everything for Christmas, a place to spend all their money and with large parking lots and masses of people shopping at 2 or 3 in the morning. There is no K-mart or Wal-mart in Cold beans. In fact, the only store is the general store and it does not stock up for Christmas. It has the same old items that are needed all the year round. Presents are hand made with love and an interest for who the present is going too. A new blanket or bed covers for someone who needs that item, Corn Cobb dolls for the girls and useful things for the boys such as new clothes, home made to fit. Cooking is big here also with the women making something to take to a neighbor for Christmas day or baking cookies or candy for the kids on Christmas morning is a standard thing.

The Christmas tree has been cut down from your own land and lovingly decorated with objects (homemade and handed down from generation to generation). Christmas is a Tradition here. It is the old ways that were handed down and taught to the kids so they can also do the same for their children in their turn as adults. Some day a store may come to Cold beans but I don't know why since we do not have money and credit cards here but it will happen and the real Christmas will be dead and the god of consumption will be born. That will be a sad day

This editor and all the mythical people who live in this town wish each and everyone a merry Christmas and a Happy New Year.

WAKE UP AMERICA

When you see a poster of America, you usually see a photo of New York City or the capital dome in Washington. This is not the true symbol of America. There are a lot more small towns than then there are big cities. Small town America is real America, not the big city. Mom, Apple pie and white churches are the true symbols we think of as America. How many of us have even seen an eagle? Look at the Norman Rockwell paintings and there is the image we believe is the true image of America. I hate to bust your bubble but alas, that is not the case.

America is losing exactly what the pilgrims came to this county to have, religious freedom, and freedom from government influence. What can you do a bout it? Not a damn thing if you sit on your duff and let it continue.. Our government starts at your door. Local government moves up to the state and the finally the nation. Never forget that "we are the people" and our voice can be heard but only if we are united in a just cause. God bless America, is only half the message, people are what makes America is he second part You don't have to run for office to make America better, but you do have to choose carefully those that represent you in the Guvmint.

COLDBEANS UPDATE

In my last letter I forgot to tell you that the state has approved the building of a bridge over Coldbeans River known to us just as the "creek". Now I know that we have no road to the creek but they want to build us a bridge so that we will know that they are working for us. Now we know that 10% of the cost of that bridge will go to our congressman. That is why they added 15% to the bill to build the bridge. A new road will be built to the bridge as soon as the mayor can get his no good son in law to build it.

There is suppose to be a sign put on the bridge saying "no diving or jumping off the bridge" but the erection of the sign will be stalled for 3 weeks so that the kids and a few of us adults can jump off the bridge and then tell people that we jumped off the bridge. There is some convoluted logic in the statement I just typed I think. I would also like to think that there is some logic in everything I write but I know that is not true.

We missed a damn good guvmint contract when they decided not to build the new prison here. Those goody two shoes that protested and said that was cruel and unusual punishment should have at least visited here before protesting the location. Heck if the prison was here some of us could visit some of our kin and not have to travel all the way to the capital city. The more things change around here the more they stay the same. That is the way we like it. Maybe after seeing our cell in the sheriff's office they thought that we could not build something that would keep the inmates inside. They might be right. We are hoping that when some of the prisoners get out they might want to stay here and make a home of Coldbeans. We would not worry about having a former crook living near us since we have a crook as mayor.

Well you have a good time in Florida and wear sunglass so that the women won't know that you are looking at them.

A MOTHER'S HAND

Sara lived right behind her mother. This was not a good thing. It seems that the family was control freaks and they checked in on Clara all the time "just to make sure that you are ok', honey". This made Sara mad as a wild cat in the creek. She wanted a life on her own. After all, she was over21 had kids and hoped someday to get married. You can be a mother, you can be a grandmother, but if YOUR parents are still alive, to them you are still a kid. A mother's apron string can stretch to the moon without breaking. There is no place "far enough away" to be out of reach of your mothers influence. No matter how well your mother raised you and trained you, you still know nothing about raising your own kids, (to the standards set by your mother that is.)

Mothers can show up on your doorstep without notice "I just thought you might need a hand with all those kids" and once she is in your home (the one that you made "just the way you like it), your mother will "make things easier to find and more better." When she finally leaves, it will take you 3 weeks to get the house back to normal. Now tell the truth, am I lying?

TO BATHE OR NOT TO BATHE

Taking a bath is not the question here, First of all, women don't mind taking a bath, but most men try to do it only once a week, with the exception of "skunk" Caleb. For him it is now twice a year. Now, for sure you have to take a bath on Sunday morning for church but women take bathing to the extreme. They want us to take a bath every day. To you city folks this may not be hard to do, after all you turn on the spigot and the water comes out, just as hot as you want. Here in Coldbeans, not many of us have indoor plumbing yet and so taking a bath is hard work. We only have one tub in the house and it is large enough for only one person to sit in and bathe. In the wintertime it is placed near the stove and in the summer, we can do it outside.

We do not change the water between people. The next person just gets in and each time the water gets a bit dirtier. Father is first (probably cause he is the dirtiest), next is Mom's turn and last are the kids. The baby always gets the dirty water and thus comes the term "don't throw the baby out with the wash water". Bathing ain't so bad. It is the dang smelly soap that the women want to use that stinks. Now, I admit that it is better than the old homemade lye soap, but it does smell wrong for a man to have on him and worse when he is around friends who can smell it and laugh at him. Well, at least once a week we can all sit and eat while smelling good and I guess it is worth the fighting.

MOTHERS DAY IN COLDBEANS

One thing wrong with working for a newspaper and especially any business is having to fire someone. Once in a while it works out for the best for both parties. We had a guy here who just could not add two numbers together even with a calculator. He could not even get to work on time and get his time card right each week. We had to let him go, but as luck would have it, the government came around and offered him a job on John Kerry's election team, as a fundraiser. Go figure.

The Coldbeans newspaper is growing larger all the time. We now have three subscribers who can't even read. They have someone read it to them. Its funny but I thought that at least Bert's wife could read.

My daughter is visiting her mother (my ex) for mother's day. She is taking her kids over to watch their grandmother's foot rot off. I figure it might take another two months for it to happen. We are going way north on Mothers day, all the way to Caesar's head mountain, in upstate South Carolina. From there we can see into Georgia and North Carolina, although I don't know why anyone would want too. We are taking the cat so if we get lost; someone will know how to get home. Rusty, the coon cat, is a very strange animal. Like most cats, he does not know he is a cat and thinks we are his furniture to sit on. We do allow him to go out on the porch and play, He came in mad as a wet hen yesterday and we found out a bird had landed on the rail and ran poor rusty off.

Well happy MOTHERS DAY to all the moms out there and hope you dads have lots of money to take them out to dinner (with the kids of course).

A FATHERS LOVE

A father is as different from a mother as night is from day. No matter if you make millions or can't find a job, to "daddy", you are his little girl and can't do wrong. "Don't worry darling, you just have not found the company that can see just how wonderful you are yet" Daddy is always there and to him you are always right and in your world daddy is the King. Dad will slip you 20 bucks at the same time that your mother is screaming about trying to make ends meet. I guess what makes dads so wonderful, is they were not attached to you as you were with your mother before birth. Moms want to give birth to a healthy baby and that responsibility starts with conception. To a dad, life starts when you come out of the womb and he can hold you and he is the one who is proud of "what he did."

God make two sexes and they are different as night and day and there is a reason for that but we just don't know what it is but it seems to work out fine. As we grow older and taller, we miss the view from a child's eyes. Why not stop and enjoy a glimpse of life on their level sometimes.

When did you last lie in the grass and stare at a buttercup or dandelion up close? When did you lie on your back and just watch the clouds drift by and try to make shapes of the different clouds? When did you stop and just smell the air and be aware that there is more to it then just breathing it? When was the last time you chewed bubble gum or drank a drink with real fruit in it, and not the artificial flavor that is popular now? When was the last time you stayed out after dark and saw a whole world of creatures that do not come out in the daylight? When was the last time you got in touch with the child inside? When will you start enjoying life instead of just living it? Stop and release the inter child and learn a new experience, one of looking at the world through a child's eyes.

For just a little while each day forget the bills, the politics, the grass to mow, the car to wash and the bills to pay and just return to the days of long ago when life was fun. We lost our imagination when TV came out, Before TV; the hero was whoever we wanted him to look like.

A CHANGED WORLD

Kids all over the world are alike, city kids, country kids, kids in Africa, Europe, Asia and everywhere there are kids, and they are alike. They like to play, to pretend they are someone or something they are not. First, for us it was cowboys and Indians. Later for our kids it was soldiers and pilots and still later, it was space men. I don't know what kids in other countries play as but America will always be known for cowboys and Indians.

If you lived in the city then Saturday was "go to the movies" at 11am and stay until supper time. In those days movies ran continuous and no break for the crowd to let out. You could see the same show over and over again. If it was a horror show, you would hide from the bad scene each time, even though you wanted to see it. It cost 10 cents to get in the movies and a nickel for popcorn and a dime for coke. A quarter went a long way then. After the show, you walked home; replaying the hero part on the way and of course, YOU were the hero!

Life was simple then; the good guy wore a white hat and would rather kiss his horse then the lady. The bad guy was mean, did not shave, and wore a black hat. Moral values have changed; the guy in the black hat now is a sadist or demented and harms innocent women. The movie is not for kids now, anyway not the kind of kids we were. We would have never gone to a sex film or a Jason film. We believed in good and evil, the cops were good and there to help you, teachers were good and the bad guys all went unshaven and smoked and wore black hats. The only dope we knew was the nutty kid up the street. Life has changed and kids had to change with it or be eaten alive by the ones that changed first. Is this a better world? Nope, not in a million years it isn't and I hope I do not live to see it get worse.

A CLOSE FAMILY

Coldbeans, being a small town, the residents are close. By that, I do not mean distance, I mean as in a family. Here when a member of the family wants to get married or live on his or her own, they inherit a bit of the family property. Thus they are on their own but also close by if needed or in need. This makes for a close relationship that binds the family together like no families in the big cities. There are exceptions to all the rules and I found that out recently while visiting a friend in Georgia.

Her family was the closest family I have met. There is the mother, matriarch of the family and then 5 children, all close, no squabble among them, close as in family and distance too. There are ten grand children, all close knit family, all love and respect each other and their parents and grandmother. This is rare in society but it does happen and many of you might be part of one or know one. In most families, there is at least one member who does not agree with the others and is the outsider but not in this family. That is a rare and wonderful thing. Many a family can't wait to get to the living apart, much less having to live in the same house.

It is the American ideal, one that is not seen often but shows up in the Norman Rockwell paintings as Americana. God bless this family and all who have the chance to know them

SPRING RAIN SHOWERS

Spring is the time for rain showers and thunderstorms. Sometimes these can be scary with the lightning zapping all around, but a gentle spring rain, late at night when you are under the cover and the rain is pitter patting on a tin roof will put you into a deep restful sleep. Even a thunderstorm, can be good. The sound of rolling thunder, rumbling thru the air far off in the distance, can be very nice. Ancient man feared the thunder and the lightning, but we here know that it is just part of spring and summer. I do not know anyone whose house was hit by lightning or even anyone that has been hit but the loud clap can still frighten people. If one is at peace with oneself then the sound of thunder can be pleasant. You can relax in your warm peaceful home safe and secure in oneself and with nature. This is just one of the many wonderful experiences of living in the country. After the storm, the air is fresh and cool and Mother Nature has had a drink of water. The flowers bloom the birds sing and all is right with the world. Our fear of nature is uncalled for. Mother Nature is our friend.

RURAL LIFE IN COLDBEANS

I know that to the outside world, Coldbeans is a hick village. Well, that is true and that is also its appeal. Sure we walk around in our "overhauls" and barefooted but that does not make us stupid. "Overhauls" are great for general wear with pockets placed just right for what you need pockets for. There is a big one in the back for your big red handkerchief to blow your nose (except we don't use them for that); we use them for wiping the sweat off our brow from working in the fields in the hot humid summer. There is a pocket for your wallet, if you need to carry one, You don't need it around the house and when you go to the general store for something, you can just tell them to "put it on the book"; knowing that for sure you will pay at the first of the month. That is our rural charge card.

There are pockets in your "overhauls" for pen or pencil; we use pencils around here. There is a place for a little notebook (not needed) and for your knife, to clean your fingernails. In other words, what we wear is for a purpose not for looks. Sure we go barefooted in the summer. Not because we are hicks but because we love to feel our toes on the green grass and smell the freshness of nature. In the winter we wear shoes (to keep from freezing our feet).

We wear a hat on our head; a straw hat is best because it lets your head breath and the heat from your head to get out. It offers shade by a large brim. Normal hats may be nice for dressing up but of no use in the fields. We are not hicks. We are smart. When we look at you in your three-piece suit out in the heat of the city which one of us is the stupid one? You have your air-conditioning to keep you cool. We have a sweet shady spot down by the creek, where we can stay cool and fish also.

There we can gather friends, catch a few catfish, drink a few beers and tell stories. Can you beat that in your cool houses?

In the summer the kids play like there is no tomorrow. But they know they have their chores too. Chores come first and then they play, very free, unrestricted and safe because we do not have here what you fear in the city. You can have all that you feel is important to your lifestyles. We love our homes, our land and our friends. In fact, we kind of feel sorry for you, because you have no idea what you are missing. Please come visit us sometime, anytime is ok for us.

MARRIAGE IN COLDBEANS

Ellie May Goodall and Joey Turnipseed decided to get married. This pleased Ellie's parents to no end, since Ellie was as pretty as a hogs butt. Of course Joey was not a good catch either, He was as dumb as a box of hammers and more useless than a drunken painter. Joey's parents were also thrilled with the wedding. Their thinking was that Joey would move in with Ellie and get out of the Turnipseed house. Meanwhile, the Goodall's were packing Ellie's bag to send her to Joey's parent's house. This was brewing to be a big disaster but in the Goodall and Turnipseed families, disaster, was common as a drink of water. The wedding was planned for a Sunday afternoon (most wedding are on Sunday. It saves one from having to get dressed up twice in one week. But this Sunday was to become hot, nasty and cause a few wrong words between people who most of the time was friends. The little white Baptist church was bright and small but the crowd who came to see this fiasco in the making was few. Most thought it would be better for them to stay home thus not having to get a bath and clean clothes to see something that would be told over the back fence anyway. Besides, staying home would save on buying a present (that cost money) and they would soon know all. These were the smart ones.

The small church is not air-conditioned, the preacher liked the idea that this was hell and she would save them to a cool nice heaven. On hot days, she could cut the sermon short and no one would complain. The people that did show up were dressed in their "go to meeting" clothes and on their best manners, prim and proper with gloves and matching pocketbook and even shoes. All the men wore ties, not because they wanted to but cause they HAD to. Besides, they did not want to miss seeing a friend (no matter how dumb he was) get into the same situation they were in but no one dare say anything to their wives or to Joey.

Well, it came the fatal hour and Ellie marched down the aisle tripped only twice and cussed only once. Joey, being sober took all this in. Ellie was wearing white, which in Coldbeans means that she was not pregnant. The veil helped but not a lot, Joey knew the face that was under the veil. The problem was that this time he was seeing Ellie while he was sober and that was something she had asked him to do. That did not help Joey. Having a hangover and getting married to an ugly girl did not help him stand there and smile. Came time for the vows and the exchange of rings and the obligatory asking "if anyone objects to this union, speak now or forever hold his piece" there ran a quiet over the church crowd. One tiny voice spoke up and said with trembling voice, "I object".

The congregation was shocked, so was the preacher and so was Ellie because the man who said it, was none other than Joey. For the first time in his whole life, he did something smart. That was the biggest fight between two families in Coldbeans in memory. After it settled, everyone went outside, ate the fried chicken and watermelon and potato salad, and got drunk on a Sunday. Ellie and Joey did not get home until dawn. So go things in Coldbeans

REMEMBER WHEN?

Remember when the good guy wore a white hat and the bad man wore black? Remember when the politician told you what HE could do for you instead of what the other guy did TO you. Remember when you got a haircut and the barber shaved your neck, with a straight razor?

Remember malt shops? Please don't ask what malt is. Remember when the preacher could come over and you were watching a program and you did not have to change the channel to avoid embarrassing him?

Well the world has changed and it took 20 years longer than George

Orwell thought it would. 1984 was a bit late. Our kids are controlled in school to keep them from selling dope or pulling a knife. They graduate so that they can fill out an application for welfare and food stamps. The government is the parent now, they tell you how to raise your kids and then when the kids go bad, it is <u>your </u>fault. Some kids eat more meals at school than at home daily.

We have DVD, Cable TV, stereo and yet there is nothing worth watching or listening to that would not embarrass everyone except the brain dead. Well at least we do not have to worry about the devil or Satan or whatever the proper term is now. Even the devil would not like this new improved world. We have no vision of the future anymore; we now have the horror of things to come. Being elected to office does not make you wiser than anyone else. Welcome to our new improved world and what will our children leave their kids?

A CHANGING WORLD

Many people think that kids of today are doomed because they do not read books; they do not write letters and have no interest in school. They think that kids only want to play on the computer, or find sites that children (and most adults) should not visit. Kids communicate more now than in the past, but they use e-mail and cell phones to do it. They are in contact with their friends everywhere, some from other states or other countries. The computer might have doomed handwriting but it made more kids want to learn the keyboard and sparked their curiosity about the world.

Remember (us old people only) when TV first came in? We were doomed to stare at that "boob tube." Television now offers something for everyone, from the intellectual to the drooling idiot. The world is changing, some think not for the better, but that is because it will be different and we are afraid of different. The world will survive, we are not smart enough yet to destroy it, but it will change, just as it has been doing for centuries. We should not try to stop this change, but we should try to prevent that when the change does come, the world and us will be ready for that change. We do not know if the future will be worse or better but that is for the kids to today to decide when they are the adults of tomorrow.

CHURCH PICNIC TIME

Believe it or not sometimes I come to this typewriter and can't find a thing to write about. Ain't no fighting going on, no one got hurt or killed, definitely no car accidents, ain't many cars here and horses got more sense than to run into each other. Bout the only thing to tell you about is some of the everyday goings on here. Some of you have written and said you would like to live here, well I don't think you would. Come visit and enjoy the difference from the city life but be assured it is not the ideal life you are used to. Sunday, after church is always picnic time and seems like every magazine shows a group of nicely dressed people standing around a table with hats on, smiles on AND a plate in the hand. In the background is this happy cook dishing up the goodies. That taint true here.

Once a month, we do have a picnic on the church grounds and there is a large oak tree to set the table under but no cooking. Picnic time is just too hot. There is home baked ham, smoke cured from the smoke house out back in someone's yard. There is the potato salad and lots of fried chicken; you just can't have a picnic with out fried chicken. We enjoy a cool watermelon when it is ripe and it is cooled by placing it in the stream and letting the cold water run over it. No ice is used.

We got sweet taters with marshmallows and iced tea. There are Lots of stewed tomatoes, picked from someone's bush last night and stewed slowly over night with okra and corn in it. There is good old green butter peas and lots of rice and chicken milk gravy. Of course, it ain't a picnic without the buttermilk biscuits on the table with fresh butter, sweet and of course cold beer.

If you got a wagon or car, you can ride home, if not, it is best to nap under the tree while the women do the cleaning up. You don't have to nap, you can lie there and open one eye and look at the cloud formations and guess what each one looks like (you are not allowed to name them after family members). Sometimes it's the peaceful things that are good to write about, we don't need the bad stuff. If we want that, we go to the big city.

AFTER THE PICNIC

WOW, what a great 4th of July party! We had a good time, no one was hurt and only one person got arrested (it was the sheriff, he had too much of his own moonshine). The food was great, the possum went quickly and the rabbit and squirrel stew with dumpling was very tasty. A couple of the boys got rowdy and threw Clem into the water but he was pretty nice about it because he had already had a bath that day for the party. Clem getting thrown into the water didn't harm any of the fish thank goodness. The best part was the greased pig contest. Horace was supposed to loan us one of his hogs for the contest but he failed to bring it to the party but a quick fix was found. One of Rafe's boys volunteered to be the pig and so we greased him up and he was hard to catch. One of his sisters managed to do it because she had the chore at home to get him to come take a bath every week and was used to chasing him.

The spiked watermelon was a hit and the pastor was caught hiding some of the seeds to take home and plant. Shame on her! There was dancing and yes some Baptist do dance but seldom in public. There was even a pie-eating contest, and an ugly kid contest that Mae-belle won with her buck teeth and freckles. Heck she wins every year. All in all, everyone enjoyed the party and hope to be over the hangover by this time next year to do it again.

GIVE TO OUR FUTURE

We do not want our children to grow up and be president some day but if that did happen, we hope that he would be a good president and when he leaves office that the country is a better place. We here raise our kids to a standard that we want to feel are the same as we want for ourselves. We try to give them the best we can within the limits of what we have to give. If we succeed only a little bit then we have added to the good of the entire community and the country and also the world. Maybe that small success will multiply with future generations and this will someday be a better world in part for the tiny bit we put into raising our children and what the rest of the country put into raising their children. There are no millionaires here, we are all dirt poor but we have a pride in self and a pride in country. We worry about wasting our vital resources, oil, coal, forest etc. The most valuable resource is our CHILDREN. We make America better by giving America better adults to mange this country. That is the mission of parents and I believe that it is in the hearts of all mothers.

MORE ON OUR PICNIC

That Fourth of July party will be one to remember. It only goes to show that the quicker you remove road kill and get in the cooler the more tender it will taste. Rabbits and coons can lie in the road a little longer and armadillo will spoil in a hurry which is why they are so expensive.

We had a show off here. Franklin Thurman was the first member of Coldbeans to own his own credit card. To celebrate, he took six of us out to the café for supper. After the meal he tossed the card to the server and say, "charges it honey". The bill came to $57.18 and after awhile she came back and told Franklin that the bill was over his limit of $50. We had to take up a collection to help him. That serves him right for being a braggart.

The sheriff had a headache for three days after the picnic; one from a hangover and two from getting bashed up side his head by his wife for going to jail drunk. If she was my wife I would drink all the time, hmmm I do drink all of the time and I am married also.

Well the world will be getting back to what we call normal for us. It is time to listen to all the lies the politicians tell us about how much good they can do US, and help themselves at the same time. We had a bad fire down at Four Holes Swamp, a nice little town near us. An apartment burned to the ground. The Church is going to send clothes to help the victims of the fire. It scares us that we are that close to death or injury by living in an apartment building and having someone accidentally burn it down. That is why in most of our homes, the kitchen is not part of the house but separated by a walk. We may lose a kitchen but not the home or our lives.

A TINY HOLE IN THE USA

On the surface, Coldbeans seems like a hole into the past. There are not a lot of small towns left that are untouched by the life styles of today. Coldbeans lies down a small two lane secondary highway, if you were not going there on purpose, you would probably pass right on by the sign and not even know that you had missed Coldbeans. We like it that way. We cling to the past because we like the life we have. If it ain't broke, don't change it. Now that does not mean that we do not have some modern conveniences, we do enjoy electricity and washing machines (those of us that have them) Of course some of our town's folks are not too keen on bathing. We have a few TV's and even though we don't have cable we are pretty lucky to get good reception on our sets.

A very few of us even have computers, now that might seem strange to you, the contradiction of modern apparatus in a rural life but some of us have gone to the big city and got an education and returned to the land of our birth to bring some new things into some of these rural ways. We don't want to change everything but we do want some progress if not for the adults then for the children who someday will fly away (hopefully) and have lives of their own. Even as I sit here in front of my desk I can reach out to the whole world. I have friends I have never met and some that I talk to every day via chat on the net. It is amazing that I can converse with people from all over the good old USA and Canada and Great Britain and Germany, Australia and Newfoundland. Anywhere someone speaks English we are able to interchange ideas. The only ones I can't talk to is the guvmint and it won't listen to me.

Communications is the key to all things in this world. It helps us understand each other and interchange new ideas. It teaches us that the world is big and there is so much out there. Our minds want to grow and need knowledge to do that. This little window is our outlet to the world and all its wonders and varied people and life styles

EATING WATERMELON

Eating watermelon is an art. You don't eat watermelon with a knife or fork, you eat it with your hands and if your mouth does not get messy then you ain't eating right. First off the watermelon must be fresh from the fields, stolen is sweeter but if you must then buy one. Take the melon to a nearby stream and place it in the shallows of a shady spot and let the cool water trickle over it for a while. Do not place it in deep water because a heavy melon will still float and you will find it way down stream.

When you think the melon is cool enough or your girl won't let you kiss her anymore, then go get the melon and slice it. Only cut the melon in half, not the dainty slices you see in stores. Watermelon should only be eaten with two things, your hands and your mouth! It will be messy and will run down your mouth and your chin but the taste is worth the mess. The good thing about a melon is that it will not stick with you it is a natural sugar and will pass. In fact, you will be "Passing" quite often as the evening goes on. The only thing in the world that can compare with a stolen and cool sweet watermelon is the girl you share it with. Pick your partner carefully. You might have to go find another melon right soon.

KIDS LEARN

There are no drugs in Coldbeans except maybe when Hattie drags her husband from the bar and home for a tongue lashing and the next morning a scrub with lye soap and a course brush. This is to clean him for going to church and is also a punishment in his own mind.

Sure, kids still smoke rabbit tobacco and drink some liquor stole from pa's stash in the wood barn but kids must explore to learn the good from the bad. Overall, we have good kids. They get in trouble, get whippings from their parents and sometimes from the neighbor who then drag them home and that means a second whipping. No hollering and screaming from the parents "you beat my boy" rather there is a thank you for helping and if you catch him doing it again whip him harder next time.

Lessons here are learned the hard way which means that sometimes sitting down is not a relaxing idea for a while after the lesson is over. No one goes to the child abuse office and no one abuses kids but when a spanking is needed, it is given, at school at home and in the neighborhood area. There is a rule, here, never spank a kid when you are mad, but when you do spank then don't let him know that you are not mad. Kids will get in trouble, they naturally want to learn and the way to learn is to try something and most time once is enough and they are satisfied to have learned that they don't like what they did. You can study books but the best lesson is hands on. Getting bit by a pig once means that you will be careful around them the next time. Falling out of a tree makes you more careful. Life is always about learning and most of it is from the school of hard knocks. Kids hate to study history. To have to learn dates and facts is boring but when grown they remember and don't mind telling their children of the wonders of the world and like when they were young, Sure, they get the blank stare and total indifference but the kids do listen. You put in a lot of knowledge and some of it will stick and be very useful when the kids grow up. They are like a garden; the quality of the crop depends on the care given when young and in the growing stage.

MOTHERS ARE THE BEST TEACHERS

Men and women think different, mothers and fathers think different. A daughter can come home to mom with three kids all under 5 and immediately, her mother takes them away and checks to make sure they are ok. It is that maternal instinct and that is something we men will never understand. Your kids can be in their 60's and you in your 80's and you will still think they are not careful enough. Let a man baby-sit and if the baby messes his or her diaper, the man will reason that it was not a lot so he can wait to change it until it is full or smells bad. If a kid drops his peanut butter and jelly on the floor, the man says, just blow on it and eat it, it won't kill you. The mother will scream, "don't eat that, it is dirty" "I will make you another one". Being a parent is something that a man has to learn from the mommies and not from books. The mother is born with the instinct and has it all her life.

Mom's teach you to wash your hands before eating, comb your hair, shine your shoes, go to church, study hard get a good job, marry and have kids of your own. Men don't worry about these things. For a boy it's, learning to shoot, chase girls and get a job. See how simple a male's life is, that is until he marries, then he has to learn all the things that his mother tried to teach him when he was young. You know what.......you gotta love them women, they are still the best companions that men have found (outside of his dog that is).

A PLACE TO PLAY

Coldbeans is like all other small towns. We have the luxury of a city park. It is small and well kept; the grass is mowed and is shown respect by its users by keeping it clean of trash. It is also the town cemetery. As strange as it seems, it works out fine, dual use of property. The adults can visit the graves and the kids have a clear area to play ball and other games.

Due to the fact that Coldbeans is fairly close to the ocean, the water table is way up, so graves are really crypts and above ground. This makes for great places for the kids to play. No disrespect is paid to the occupants. In fact if they could talk, I think they would be delighted to see the children romp and squeal over where they lay. Over head there are some of the most beautiful trees in the area. Great oaks with Spanish moss hanging majestically and looking like graybeards of the confederacy. Crepe myrtle's (from which Myrtle Beach gets it name) bloom like it is their last chance to show off. Large azaleas also compete for this show of brilliant colors. Walk through the winding oyster shells paths and you will hear small voices above you. Don't worry, the local people know from whence come these little voices. These same adults have hidden in the tops of these same trees as kids and teased the passer byes with childish delight.

Buried in the crypts are some of the leaders of this community and also some of the very bad guys. Cemeteries have a way of making everyone equal. Lying here are some confederate rebels, and also some bluecoats that once fought each other and now share a common place of peace. This we should reflect on (if we can be at peace in death, would it not be more worthwhile, to be at peace in life)? Looking at the children's faces and eyes we should be able to see the innocence of youth and that the real purpose of life is the getting along with each other. Kids see other kids as people to play with, not as different in color or value.

OTIS AND JOSHUA

Joshua and his wife lived in a small shack on the back of Otis's property. Now Joshua was a black man, Otis was white, and everyone knew that Otis did not cotton to black people but for some reason he let Joshua and his wife live on the property. Otis went to church weekly and most Sundays Joshua and his wife went also but in separate wagons. Some times when Marlene was ill Joshua went and sat in the back row most of the times by his self. Otis was a deacon and sat in the front row dressed in his best suit. Times were bad then, crops were not good and most days were lean picking for something to eat. Joshua and Marlene rarely had much to eat.

Otis came round to see Joshua several times a month and said hello. He was polite but not real friendly. He was just a neighbor who was checking on a neighbor. One time Joshua invited Otis in for a meal. It was not much, just some boiled turnips and potatoes, the plates were clean, and the table was set with the best Joshua had.

A few days later, Joshua went outside to feed his all too lean pigs and on the porch was a frozen half side of beef. There was no note from who ever put it was there, a nice lean beef. No one knows where it came from, except that Joshua did notice that one of Otis/s cows were missing and that could mean that Otis killed a cow for his own use or maybe…? No one will ever know, but Joshua never went hungry again. Sometimes church does things to a man and makes him a better person for the deed.

BRAGGING RIGHTS

Stupid is the norm around Coldbeans. This is not from being "unlearned" but from being unable to learn. That defect does not bother most parents since having a smart kid might confuse the adults. It is hard to teach someone who is already smarter than you will ever be. It is possible and we know of one example where the idiot of the family is the smarted of all of the family. That is one family that should quit breeding.

It is not a shame to have an idiot in the family. There is always the hope that he will grow up and become a politician. The family can then brag that their son is the biggest idiot in the state capital but they don't tell people that by biggest they mean that the son has to have his clothes made by Omar the tent maker. This is proof that it is not what you say but the way you phase it. After all some of the prettiest weeds grown from cow pies (if you don't know what that is go visit a farm and walk around barefooted. Cow pies will cure athlete's foot. Rubbing it on your head will not cure stupid though.

Having the idiot of the family helps all the relatives feel better about their branch of the family. They can't brag about their son being smarter but they can brag about their son being less dumb than the kin's. There are other ways to brag about your kids. Just tell the neighbor that your kids smell better than their hogs do. Of course that is only cause your kids take a bath more often then their hogs do.

Even if "up" is not far away just being up more up than the neighbor makes you feel right proud. There is often a good possibility that your kid might marry the next door girl (after the baby is born and you can see who it looks like). Then you will be part of one big happy family and even maybe friends too.

CANING DAY

Around Coldbeans, the saying 'the sap is rising" does not mean sugar maple time but the man of the house is getting up and where is his breakfast. The wives of these "saps" coined this saying. Although we do not have sugar maples and maple syrup except when you buy it in the general store we do have "sugarcane time" Sugar cane time is in the fall.

It is equally as interesting as maple time but occurs at a different time of the year. Of course many communities do not do it as much as we do, but we are old fashioned. We do our own cane unlike the people who grow cane and send it to a processing plant to be made into syrup. There are large fields of cane and at the right time, the workers go into the field with "strippers." These are tools to remove the leaves from the cane. These leaves are razor sharp and can do a wicked cut on you also. Then the workers go in with the machetes and cut the cane. Sugar cane looks like bamboo and you cut it close to the ground. Down here the cane will grow again in the next season.

The cane is carried to the mill. The mill is a tall pillar with a pole sticking out to harness the mule up to. He goes round and round and never gets dizzy or lost. While this is happening, you gather some of the cane and stick it into the slots in the mill. As the mill turns, it squeezes the juice out of the cane and into a vat. This juice is then cooked over a fire and the whey is skimmed off and given to the hogs. They get so drunk from it that they fall down with their tongues sticking out. The syrup is reduced until it is thick and ready to be cooled and bottled or jugged. Cane syrup has a bit of a tart flavor with a little molasses to it. If you are raised on it, it is gooood but if you are raised on maple syrup don't try it. Not all of the cane is made into syrup; some of it is cut up and stored as silage for the cows and hogs. It is sweet and puts weight on them in a hurry.

DIVORCE IN COLDBEANS

Essie May caught her husband, Elmer once again at the Hot House dance saloon. She caught him red handed. He was caught dancing with one of the girls and trying to make a "spend the night" deal. Someone called the doctor so he could be at Essie's place when she got Elmer home. He was not hurt (she never hurts him when he is drunk because he can't feel anything then). She was waiting for him to sober up so she could whip the tar out of him. She never wanted to divorce him, that would make him happy and besides she enjoyed making his life a reign of eternal terror. Essie was not a sweet woman and few understand why he married her except he could not find a sane woman that would say yes.

Marriage and divorce are the same all over the world. There are slight differences in the city and the towns. Small towns like Coldbeans seem to have fewer divorces but beneath us there are more unhappy marriages. In a large city, divorce is so common that it is hardly noticed except for the wife, husband and children. A few neighbors may gossip and say quietly, "well I knew it would not last" and also the parents of the bride says "I told you it was wrong". Other than that it is commonplace but not in Coldbeans. Coldbeans, being a small place, everyone knows everyone and what they are doing and with whom they are doing it. There are no secrets. If a husband is a drunken lazy lout, all know and if the wife is a shrew, mean, does not keep a good house then all know that too.

People in small towns stay together because they are in for the long haul and most try to work things out or just fool around on the other person. Sometimes, this solves the problem because if caught, one or more can end up dead. Marriages can be the right choice at the time that it occurs but many years down the road, people evolve or change. Taste and habits are not the same, no one is bad, cruel, or cheating, it is just that they can't stand each other anymore and the adult thing to do is part (as friends if possible). If there are kids, they will still be the kids of both parties, dad will be dad and mom will still be mom. The roles will not change, just the location where they live.

Around Coldbeans, it is not unusual for the husband to just build another house on the same property and live near by, family is important to people here. Being as it is his own house; he can drink, and smoke, walks around naked and scratch his butt when he wants. Sometimes this life style gets old and the two end back up with each other and both aware that two people jointly become one couple united. This is the good ending. The flip side is one of anger, fighting, getting drunk and landing in jail. Then this marriage will not be anymore. Both parties are better off not seeing each other. Sometimes, the dumb people of the small town are not that dumb after all.

DOUBLE UGLY

Lipstick and makeup is not a big item in Coldbeans. It is a waste of good money trying to make some of our women look like women. Have you noticed that some of the ugliest women in the world have a bathroom full of beauty aids? There is skin softener, wrinkle remover, hair treatments and other things that we men are not suppose to know about. Putting makeup on some women is like putting lipstick on a hog and the only time I know of that happening was one time when "skunk" Caleb got so lonely that he tried it I don't think that even his now dead wife ever kissed him, or if she did, it was done while she held her breath.

Make up is not a big seller in the general store here. Most of the women here know they are "plain" looking and they don't even try to hide it. After all if you pretty yourself up for a man and then he gets "lucky" and the next morning when the sun comes up and he turns over in the bed and sees the real thing he might go screaming butt naked out the door. Now there is nothing wrong with trying to make you look better but for some of us it is like brushing the head of a bald man. You got to have something to work with first. The sage once said "to one's own self be true" If you are ugly you cannot help that, but being a fake is trying to fool the other people.

ENJOY THE CHILD INSIDE

As we grow older and taller, we miss the view from a child's eyes. Why not enjoy a glimpse of life on a different level. When did you lie in the grass and stare at a buttercup or dandelion up close? When did you lie on your back and just watch the clouds drift by and try to make shapes of the different clouds? When did you stop and just smell the air and be aware that there is more to it then just breathing it? When were the last time you chewed bubble gum or drank a drink with real fruit in it, and not the artificial flavor that is popular now? When was the last time you stayed out after dark and saw a whole world of creatures that do not come out in the daylight? When was the last time you got in touch with the child inside?

When will you start enjoying life instead of just living it? Stop and release the inter child and learn a new experience, one of looking at the world through a child's eyes. For just a little while each day, forget the bills and the politics, the grass to mow, the car to wash and the bills to pay and just return to the days of long ago when life was fun. We lost our imagination when TV came out. Before TV, the hero was whatever we wanted him to look like. The good guy won and did not sleep with the lady and also was faithful to his horse. Return to the days of yesterday before pollution and chemicals and dangers to children at the park, at school and at play. Return to your own childhood; take a vacation from the adult world and I think you will want to return time and time again once you have visited.

THE ICE CREAM PARLOR

I will bet that we have something here in our little town that you don't have in your big city (besides peace and quiet). We have an ice cream parlor. Not one of those places that sell 50 flavors and the scoops are tiny but a real parlor with good old homemade ice cream. It is run by two ladies' that wanted to have part of their past remembered. Now you think that "home made" might lead to people wondering if it is good, is it safe to eat and how does it taste? Well come on in and sit a spell and try a dish of the best peach, chocolate, strawberry or vanilla ice cream you ever locked a lip on. It is cold, but not hard as a rock. That makes it creamy and fun to eat. It has only the ingredients that nature makes and nothing artificial. If you get it in a cone, you want to go outside where everyone can watch you lick the soft sweet stuff and of course suck the melting ice cream from the bottom of the cone. Kids are not the only ones sitting with their feet up and leaning back with a good old cold cone and a cute gal beside them. The real old fashion banana split lives here also. The real thing, with 3 scoops, one with chocolate, one with strawberry and one with vanilla, covered with pineapple, chocolate syrup and strawberries and lots and lots of whipped cream and chopped nuts on top. Bring someone to carry you home cause you ain't gonna feel like walking after eating all that.

The ice cream is churned by hand and there are many customers to add a hand to help. Mostly though, there are kids who get paid to do this chore and they do get to sample for free. Ah! Summer with an ice cream cone and sitting outside under the elm tree and watching the black smith making music with his hammer and anvil is like nothing in the big city! There are even cakes and pies to take home, all hand made by the best cooks in the town. Sorry but you can keep the big city, I think I will stay here

HOME DECORATING, COUNTRY STYLE

It is bad enough when the women want to plant flowers to "beautify" Coldbeans, but when\ it comes to doing the house we run like a scalded dog. Klara, (I know and you know it is spelled Clara but she thought she was the social butterfly of Coldbeans and came up with a new idea.

Now if she had watched some of these makeover shows, she would have known the idea was not new but properly done can be tasteful. She went begging and whining to a lot of carpet stores in the surrounding area and got a lot of sample squares. She had been told to start placing the squares from the middle of the room and work towards the walls and all would be good. In fact, it did look good (about like an explosion in a paint factory0! She asked how we liked it and I am glad the preacher was not there because we lied and said "it looks wonderful"

Now, you know women, If one does something, another has to do better. Tallied went to all the markets in the surrounding country and gathered up the square cartons that eggs come in, not the dozen kind but the big square one, called flats. She took them home and spray painted them all different colors and stapled them to the walls. If a blind drunk saw them, he would go screaming and running out the door and never drink again. It was a sight to make for sore eyes, and it was a real test to not laugh. One day rumor has it that a chicken got into the house and killed herself trying to lay enough eggs to fill the wall.

ONLY STREET

People have asked (I don't know why) what the name of the main street is in Coldbeans? Well for a long time it was the only street in Coldbeans that was paved so the name "Only Street" stuck. There are other roads, not called streets because at the time they came into being, they were unpaved but are really wide lanes and not streets. There is sheriff's Lane, named cause it goes to his house and blacksmith lane cause that is where he works. Schoolhouse road is where the schoolhouse teacher lives and teaches and sometimes gets a bit drunk but rarely does anyone see him that way but when he does get drunk we can understand it. If I was a teacher, I would stay drunk all the time.

The names of the lanes are practical and came into being cause it was easy to give directions that way. Most of the businesses in Coldbeans are on Only Street. The sheriff is located behind the barbershop and that is convenient, he can sleep out side and no one notices. If you are just passing thru look quickly cause we ain't no big city. We don't even have a stoplight that works anymore.

KEEPING WARM IN WINTER

Heating the home was at one time quite a chore. There was no oil heater or gas heat. We had only the kitchen stove to warm in the winter and for some there was the good old potbelly stove or cannon heater. The potbelly stove was a good heater and would put out heat but it did have its faults. If you were too close, you got HOT. If you were not lucky to get close on cold night, it was a bit chilly. Heat does not radiate equally. You had to keep wood or coal in it. Wood was free, just cut it. Coal cost you money and cost to deliver also so that meant wood was the fuel of choice. The best heater was the kitchen stove. It both heated and cooked and had a place to heat water for a bath. This too had its drawbacks, in the summertime it was hard to live in the kitchen.

In the real old days, the kitchen was not part of the house. This was just common sense. If you had a house fire, most times it started in the kitchen. It was easier to rebuild a kitchen rather than rebuild the whole house. The very best warmer was mom's bed with her feather comforter. It was light but oh so warm underneath it. You could keep everything warm but your nose. We lost something when we went to central heat. Have a nice day

THE GOOD OLD OUTHOUSE

One of the things that you would not like that we had to contend with was where to put the toilet. On very cold nights we kept a "slop jar" under the bed or somewhere near by. Having to put on clothes and shoes to run to that little house with the half moon in the dead of winter was not something we liked to do drunk or sober. The slop jar was not a healthy thing but was useful. The outhouse was a better deal but was not heated, not comfortable and also you could not read if you wanted to use it during the dead of the night. The best way was to train yourself to wait till daylight if you could. Now it does get cold here in the winter, but it also gets powerfully hot here in the summer and this was the other problem. At least on a cold night the smell was not too bad. Someone got the bright idea of a trap door in the roof that would open and let out the bad air and let in some light. This was NOT useful on a rainy day. The old joke about the sears catalog was true but other methods worked also. Corncobs were plentiful and worked but were painful. No one said that the "good ole times" were always fun. That was just the way of life at that time and we did not know of the things that are taken for granted in this age.

HOW TO BUY A USED CAR

One of the hardest things to do and do it right is to buy a car or truck. Never buy a new one, it is not new once you get it off the lot so buy a used one and save money. Get a car that you can work on without a lot of cost to you.

First, find a car with a large trunk. This is so that in the winter when you have no job, you can haul cord wood for people and the larger the trunk, the more you can get in there and the more you make on each trip. Get a car with a good rear view mirror. Nothing looks worse than a nice pair of wooly dice hanging from a cheap mirror and you can also spot the law a longs ways off then. Change the horn; get one that makes music as it toots. If you need to replace body parts, never buy a part the same color, it will not look right. Get another color (on a red car, a nice white hood will do fine). Good tires are necessary but the rims should cost at least twice as much or more than the tires and at least as much as the car. Over size wheels on high struts work well here.

If you are a teenager then a loud stereo is required but if you are an adult and halfway sane, you will find that the stereo will take up too much room and you will not be able to get much cordwood in the car. The engine is not important as long as it works. The muffler is of great importance. It must be loud and make everyone notice you as you go by. The way to know if you got the right deal is if no daddy will let their daughter ride with you at any time. Never drive your truck to the insurance company for them to take a look at. If you do, be prepared for very high premiums or cancellation. Follow these simple guidelines and you will have a truck that the guys will beg to ride in and every police car in town will want to follow you around.

YOUR OPPONENT IS ALWAYS A BIGGER LIAR THAN YOU ARE

Why do we elect the president from a list of the LEAST WORSE of the Candidates? No one talks about what he or she can do but what the other slime ball did. This is not unique to this country; politicians in all countries who are elected do so by putting down the other fellow. To paraphrase a former president "asks not what your country can do for you, ask what my opponent did to you." We should aspire to great goals not muckrake. It is sad that politics are about dirty laundry and not noble ideas. Everyone has a toilet in their house and uses it but we do not need to know how often they use it. Politics are about what the other guy did and why you didn't do it to... Watching politicians on TV during election time is sad, even football is better to watch. Millions of dollars are spent on complains to tell you how the other side is wasting money and not helping the poor. No politician will tell you how wonderful America is; it is only how awful this country is because of the other party's doings.

Show me a candidate who will be positive in his views and not drag down his opponent and I will vote for him, no matter which party he might be for. It is a reality and a joke that we expect our representatives to be crooked. How can you expect someone to be honest if you yourself ain't too? Once America was the envy of the world, now we are in debt to the people that we used to lend money to and not expect it back? Remember the song that the British played at their surrender to America? It was "the world turned upside down" Well we had better start learning that song. Some points are best made thru illustration. So here is the tale of the fly and the wagon.

A fly thought that he was very smart. Anytime the farmer when to town the fly would hitch a ride. This saved him the energy of using his wings. The fly would watch and when the wagon was hitched up and the farmer got into the wagon and picked up the reins, the fly would go down and light on the front of the wagon tongue. The horse, laden with the load the farmer was taking to town, would sweat and strain at the load. The fly, meanwhile, would ride in comfort on the front of the pole, with the wind in his wings and the sun on his back.

The horses did not like the job of pulling the wagon, especially on the hills around the area and the many deep ruts in the road.
He also did not like the idea that the fly was riding for free and told him so. The fly answered back to the horses, "Why do you complain" "I am doing all the work as you can see"

Moral, "the effort is not in the doing, it is who seems to be doing the doing"

SKUNK'S SPRAY

"Skunk" Caleb almost made an important discovery, not on purpose. He ain't that smart but found this though his not bathing often. "Skunk" is famous for his smell. Unlike us common folks around here, "Skunk" has no roaches in his house. Logical deduction (by "skunk") is that the smell drives them away. There might be something to that; "skunks" smell sure drives us away. Like all good ideas (such as the 8 track player) not all ideas prove to be beneficial. You can use roach spray to ward off roaches, but there is no spray for the smell of Skunk. Besides roaches hide in the daytime, but the image of "skunk" is forever. Three terrorist countries have offered to pay "skunks" way over there to analyze and bottle his smell for uses they won't tell. Only problem was that the airlines would not fly him and the boats would not book him, so he said "to hell with it" "Skunk" must be smarter than he looks, He sure is smarter than he smells, I know that.

NEW DEPUTY

Coldbeans has a new deputy to assist sheriff Bubba. Now bubba is not the sheriff's real name but all sheriffs in the south are called bubba. In fact, most of the men in the south are known as bubba's. The deputy is more than just an assistant to the sheriff; he is also the most beloved town drunk of southern towns. If you gotta have a deputy, get one that knows the town and the jail and is there when needed. Harley knows everyone that is arrested. Some of them are kin to him and the rest have dated Harley's sister. Harley is not allowed to help with the sideline moonshine business that the sheriff runs. Harley is tempted to sample the wares and does not have good taste. If the brew gets him drunk, it is ok by him but the sheriff has a class clientele and they want only the good stuff.

Harley has the keys to the jail door, locks himself up daily, and is free to patrol the town at night and being an "official" he gets to sample the wares of the businesses. Al in all, it works out fine, Harley works for room and board and has a get out of jail free card but has never used it. Maximize the potential in everyone you know, put their talents to good use and get the most for the least cost. That is the motto of our town jail and its sheriff.

NO NEWS IS GOOD NEWS HERE

To some of you people from the big cities, some of our news may seem tame or boring. We prefer to think of it as being well off and we always like happy news over all that bad stuff you get in your papers. We have no traffic jams, no stoplights and no pedestrian crossings. Matter of fact we walk on any side of the road we want and even in the middle of the road if no horses or cars are a coming. We don't need stop lights cause our drivers are polite and yield to others and we tip our hats to the women who usually blush at the attention. The general store in town is mostly for the men. We stand round and talk about what I am writing about right now. So what is in this paper is not news to the town, just to you people.

We had two new kids born in town and it was almost tragic. Seems the father to be was on the way to the hospital and crashed into a ditch and was unconscious when the babies (one boy one girl) were born. Well it's a tradition here that when children are born they are right away named but with the dad out of it, the chore fell to his brother, the kid's uncle. Upon awaking, the new mom asked what the names of the children were since it was her brother-in-law that named them and he was as bright as a burned out bulb. The kids' uncle said that he had named the girl Denise, which is kind of a nice name. The boy he called de nephew.

More bad news, Doug's hogs got out again and came to town. Believe it or not, they were hanging around the slaughterhouse (probably looking for some of their kin). Well you all have a good day and a better tomorrow. Bye for now

NEVER A LENDER OR BORROWER BE

Keeping in touch and never a lender or borrower be is ok for city folks, but here it is necessary and a natural part of life. Borrowing is a necessary thing. We don't all have the things that we need, such as a bottom plow, or a large wash tub and who wants to spend good money on something that is seldom used. Someone in the neighborhood will have what you need, no matter what it is. All you have to do is ask someone and they will tell you where to go to get that it. That is just being neighborly and the other important part is returning the item when through with it, clean and in the same shape as when you got it. This works for everything but children. No one borrows kids unless it is to help with a chore and then they are rewarded with something nice, not money but maybe cake or ice cream.

That insurance company ain't the only good neighbor. No neighbor will turn down the asking for a favor unless they don't have that item or the time to do the chore that you ask. Even then they will volunteer the name of someone who can help you with that problem. This makes for good neighbors but doe not help the poor guy down at the general store. Being a good neighbor is making him very poor but after all, he too borrows from the neighbors. You might say that in Coldbeans, not everyone is kin (most are) but they ALL are family

A TALE OF THREE MOTHERS

Everyone loves their mother, no matter if she was good or bad. She was Mother or for the lucky people that still have a mother she is MOM. This is a special tribute to my mothers, yes plural, cause I am a lucky man to have three moms

I did not know my first mother, she died when I was about two but I do know from the others that she loved me and played with me every chance she got but God called her and she had to leave and so the only MOM I knew was my Grandmother, who I thought was my mother. As a young boy starting school I did note that all the other kids had young mothers but mine was old. What the heck, at 6 how was I to know that some moms are not old, She loved me and cared for me and I called her mom but she was old, and old is not good for raising a 6 year old who gets into the troubles that a kid gets into when exploring the world.

I would get into trouble at school and have to take a note home and I would cry all the way home. She did not whip me. She understood and I was punished as a child must be but without violence. I was made to sit in a chair and stay there. For an active child this is horrible punishment. I remember one time crying my self to sleep sitting in the chair and when I dosed off, I fell forward and I woke up just as my grandmother caught me. She had been watching over me all the time. As she and I got older, she was less capable of caring for me and I was into many things, most of which I should not have been in. The police station was across the street and they saw that she was not capable of caring for me so I was placed in the orphanage. To a 9 year old this was a terrible place. There was no mother to come to for hugs and security. I was miserable and missed "mom" but looking back on it, it was a great time to be a boy. We were on the water and we could fish or crab or swim, and we could run barefoot and carefree.

After two years, my aunt and uncle took me out and cared for me until I grew up, but I had been scarred. I was very insecure and was afraid that I could be sent back to that place at any time. My aunt and uncle treated me as if I was their own but I wanted my mommy. I missed my "mother" To those who still have moms please love them for as long as you can,

WHAT IS REALLY IMPORTANT

Remember when there was a storm and the electricity went off? You sat in the dark and you could feel the cold or the heat according to the season. Nothing worked, the stove, the radio, the TV, the clocks or the lights. We become accustom to these things.

Later in life I have seen houses (not homes) where the farm workers in California were "living" while working their way to the northern part of the state. They kept warm around a 50 gallon drum with a fire made of anything they could find. It would be cold and the girls would be in light dresses and the boys barefooted. This is real and it is not made up. This was in Bakersfield, California in the 60's and I still remember it. These people had only the barest of living comfort, maybe a bed but probably it was one in the cabin rented for the time they were there. There were no lights, no heat and no hope of getting any. There was no hope of the lights coming on after the storm had gone by. It was a way of life and all they knew. They were only surviving I say all of this because I am sitting here with a defective modem in my computer and will get a new one tonight. I miss the contact with the rest of the world and all my friends, but I know that unlike the kids in Bakersfield many years ago that I will have contact again. This is only temporary. What are the things that are important in your life? Are they REALLY important? Could you do without them? Sure you would miss them but you would survive. We in America have become spoiled with our many trinkets and think that the whole world lives just like we do, nice house, two kids, a dog, TV and indoor plumbing. We can dream of a future but many in this world can only hope they make it thru the night and wake up the next morning. Maybe my modem is not that important and maybe I can find other things to do for awhile because I have the luxury of knowing that I can and will get a new one, but it does make you reflect on what is really important

4TH OF JULY PARTY TIME

The fourth of July is fast approaching and we are preparing for the grand festivities. We did lose some of the road kill stored at Abe's but most of it is still good and with a little seasoning, you won't even taste the tainted flavor. We also plan to have some special treats provided by the women of the church. We will be having okra on a stick and watermelon. Doc Hines is donating a bottle of vodka and several needles for injecting the watermelon. Remember no spiking the punch this year. Last year three women from the church were arrested for drunk walking. The sheriff has donated the use of his three prisoners to help with setting up the tables and collecting the money for the dinner. Don't worry; none of the men are in jail for stealing. Well, one is but that was for an apple pie that was left on the windowsill of Ms Slocomb's house. That ain't stealing, it is only testing tasting.

Clem, Abe and Caleb will be marching with the American, South Carolina and Confederate flag. We picked them cause them are the only ones who can stay in step with the music. Remember to take off your hat when the flags pass by. Clem's ex-wife promised she will give him a bath before the big day. She could use some help cause Clem don't like baths you know and she has not told him about it yet.

The party will be held down at Lake Stumpy and remember there will be no nude swimming this year. Last year was mentioned in the sermon for three Sundays in a row. No tobacco spitting at the dinner table and no eating with your hands (except the watermelon). Remember, Ladies will be present and so will the kids. Anyone catching fish at the lake is welcome to fry them right there and share with friends. Caleb is towing his outhouse down to the site for the women. The men can use the oak tree down from the creek. We hope everyone enjoys the party this year and no one get hurt while drunk

INBREEDING?

We have several families here that are no kin to each other, thru parent, cousins or marriage. Their kids are idiots, now how do you account for that? If two people kin to each other have kids, does it have to mean that the kids will be idiots? Can't just once in a while a brother and sister or cousin have intelligent children? Does inbreeding mean that your kids have a better chance of getting elected to a political position than the SOB's that are in office now? If inbreeding produces idiots then why is this town not full of them? It they were all idiots, then there would be no one to read this paper or even write it, nuf said, fact proven!

HOLLYWOOD WISDOM

Many of you readers think that Coldbeans is a rural town full of stupid people. Rural is right but stupid they are not. The fact that we live outside of the main stream does help us get a clearer sight on the realities of the world. We want to know why people who act for a living, who pretend to be someone they are not and read a script and of course make a lot of money for it, all of a sudden become the guru of wisdom and knowledge. People who cannot think for them selves feel that what some actor or actor in Hollywood says or thinks should be the correct wisdom for the world. If there is a den of evil, Hollywood is it. They have taught us how cool it is to be a druggie, how to drop out of school, that it is ok to be gay and that you should flaunt it to the world and make the world think as you think.

Money is not wisdom or intelligence. There are lots of people that are wise beyond what the spoiled brats in Hollywood think. Many of these people work hard and some have little schooling but they know what they know from the realities of living in the real world, not the false reality of Hollywood. Hanoi Jane and all you phony self-appointed smart people would lead this Country to socialism in a minute. "From the cradle to the grave, let us think for you cause we know best and you are not smart enough to think for yourselves".

God bless those that think for themselves and not do as told by the phony gurus of the Babylon in California

FLY PAPER AND OTHER THINGS

You have to be old to remember flypaper and fly strips. No matter how careful you were a few flies would get into the house. Stores had the strips hanging from the ceiling and so did cafes where the food would attract them. By today's standards, they would be banned as unsanitary but back then, they were a necessary evil. We were accustomed to many things back then that we take for granted now. On a cold morning, someone had to get up and start the fire so the kids would be warm to dress for school; (yes we had school way back then). You kids of today think there was no school in our time because history had not been invented back then.

We also had something else that is missing from today. We had <u>ethics</u> and loyalty to those who we worked for and the company that was good to us. It was a career and you worked as many years as you wanted to, no kicking you out when you got old and near pension time. There were no food stamps; no welfare and drugs were the grounds in the bottom of the coffee pot. There are a lot of good things about today. People are treated lot more equal and we have things that could only be dreamed of back then but we have lost the caring sprit of being a good neighbor. Was it really worth the trade off?

ETTA SUE AND THE BABY

Etta Sue was the most popular girl in school at least with the boys. She was not that well liked by the girls because all the boys liked her. Etta was friendly with all the boys, (to use a polite word) in the 10th grade thru senior class. She had dated all eight of the boys on the football team (it was a small school and could not field the whole eleven required by football standards). She even had dated most of their brothers and one of the coaches. None of the boys were jealous. In fact, when one of the young guys finally got interested in girls Etta Sue was the first girl they set him up with. After a date with Etta Sue, most of the boys were more confident in their ability to relate to the opposite sex. Now as it happens, if you cast your hook in the water often enough, you do catch a fish. In

Etta Sue's world, the problem was whose bait was it? She had so many potentials to choose from.

Etta Sue might be what you call "round heeled" but she was smart and she knew that whatever boy she picked he would think that he was the right one. The problem was she did not know who the baby would look like when it was born. This decision took a lot of pondering. Etta Sue chose wisely. The young lad stuck with the responsibility for being the father and for helping raise the baby was named Robert Joe, a very bright young lad and he was good looking too. He never suspected that he was chosen by his qualifications to be a good father and husband, rather than for being the real father.

Etta and Robert were married and her parents were so proud and all the rest of the young men in the town were happy too and also were greatly and silently relieved. Etta, Robert, and little Bobbie, were a perfect family. The same energy Etta put into being a good lover she put into being a good wife. She was faithful to her husband and he loved and adored her and felt like he was the luckiest man in town.

Most of the other men felt luckier than Robert but he did not know that and they did not tell him. Robert turned out to be a good catch, He went on to College and started his own business, and the small family moved from Coldbeans to the "big" town. No one there knew of her past. They were well liked, and strangely, the baby did look somewhat like Robert. The moral of this is that what you don/t know does not always hurt you, if fact, it can be a good thing.

IDIOTS OR GENIUS

It is a thin line between Idiot and Genius. Here in Coldbeans the line sometimes is blurred. Jumbo got a brilliant idea, something that he rarely gets and brilliant ones never but this time he might have hit on something. Jumbo hated to have to go out on cold mornings and get firewood for the potbelly stove. He also hated that the room that the stove was in, was too hot and the others were a bit too cold. Being one of Coldbeans more clever people he knew that the pipe venting the smoke out got hot and helped heat the room.

Jumbo went to the store and almost bought them out of stovepipe. He ran the pipe from the potbelly all the way to the back of the house, and up near he ceiling. His thinking was that the heat would radiate from the pipe and make the whole house warm and toasty. It worked well, the whole family slept toasty that night; well most of the night that is. They over slept the next morning and the stove went out due o lack of attention, meaning fuel. It had felt so warm under the covers that not anyone wanted to be the one to go get more wood for the stove.

Don't ask why they did not think of storing more wood inside the night before. A genius cannot think of everything. The idea of using all the heat worked though. It was not long before he had pipes thru the ceiling of the whole house and by the time the smoke out of the house, the smoke was cold and the people inside were warm.

For every good there must be a bad to equal things out. Sure it was warm, but his wife did not like the idea of pipes everywhere and the pipes had to be dusted often, meaning more work for her. Meanwhile Jumbo sat and enjoyed the warmth. Everyone that was affected by that idea did not accept it as a good idea.

RURAL LIFE IN COLDBEANS

I know that to the outside world, Coldbeans is a hick village. Well, that is true and that is its appeal. Sure we walk around in our "overhauls" and barefooted but that does not make us stupid. "Overhauls" are great for general wear with pockets placed just right for what you need pockets for. There is a big one in the back for your big red handkerchief to blow your nose (except we don't use them for that); we use them for wiping the sweat off our brow from working in the fields in the hot humid summer. There is a pocket for your wallet, if you need to carry one. You don't need them around the house and when you go to the general store for something, you can just tell them to "put it on the book"; knowing that for sure you will pay at the first of the month. That is our rural charge card.

There are pockets in your "overhauls" for pen or pencil; we use pencils around here. There is a place for a little notebook (not needed) and for your knife used to clean your fingernails. In other words, what we wear is for a purpose not for looks. Sure we go barefooted in the summer. Not because we are hicks but because we love to feel our toes on the green grass and smell the freshness of nature. In the winter we wear shoes to keep from freezing our feet!!!! We wear a hat on our head; straw is best because it lets your head breath and the heat from your head to get out. It offers shade by it's large brim. Normal hats may be nice for dressing up but is of no use in the fields. We are not the hicks, we are smart. When we look at you in your three-piece suit out in the heat of the city which one of us is the stupid one?

You have your air-conditioning to keep you cool. We have a sweet shady spot down by the creek where we can stay cool and also fish a bit. We can gather friends and catch a few catfish and drink a few beers and tell stories with each other Can you beat that in your cool houses?
In the summer the kids play like there is no tomorrow. They do have their chores too. Chores come first and then they play, very free, unrestricted and safe because we don't have here what you fear in the city. You can have all that you feel is important to your lifestyles. We love our homes, our land and our friends. In fact, we rather feel sorry for you because you have no idea what you are missing. Please come visit us sometime. Anytime is ok for us.

AINT NO FIGHTING OR FUSSING HERE

You might notice that I have not mentioned any fighting going on in Coldbeans. That is true. If there is family fighting, it is behind closed doors and not the throw the husband and the pots and pans out the door thing. Most husband here are smart enough to keep their mouth shut when they know they can't win the argument. Who ever heard of A husband wining anything? People have so much work to do that they don't have the energy left over for fighting and there ain't any argument over TV, football or other sports. I have heard of a few kids getting their rations cut off from doing wrong things but never child abuse. Kids here know right from wrong and it they do wrong they know that there is a coming punishment waiting. School lessons, field chores, helping with the dishes and helping with the smaller kids are all part of life and expected of them. If ever the sheriff goes out to visit a house for a drunken husband then most times a talking to is usually all that is needed, but sometimes, one night at the jail will make him sober and wiser. I think you city folks would get bored here after awhile.

DOC AND THE HIGHWAY PATROL

"Doc" drove to the big city about once a week. Now, "doc" was not a doctor, it was just an honorary title because everyone thought he knew everything. Doc had a special car. Since he missed his right leg, and the car was straight shift, he had a contraption to put on the clutch when he stepped on the brake. This handicap did not stop him from burning up the road. The drive to the big city on a weekly basis was a boring one. Doc tried to get all the speed he could each time and spending less time in the car, the more time for work meant the faster he got home.

Now, our highway patrols here frowns on speeding. It was a sure bet that eventually he would be caught. It happened, not once but three times on the same trip home. The first time, the Deputy was nice and let him off with a warning since he was a handicapped driver. The second cop was not as nice and Doc got a healthy ticket for 50 bucks and a chewing out, which made doc later to get home and a bit angrier. The third cop had the bad luck of stopping Doc very shortly after the second time and while doc was still fuming over the other two incidents. When the cop came to the window, Doc was not too cooperative. Now in SC you do not get angry with a highway patrol officer. You just cannot win and you could end up in jail. Doc was lucky again, being handicapped; the officer just gave him another ticket and a warning.

That was when Doc messed up, "he told he officer that "he knew how to drive the damn car" and he was being held up for no reason at al." The highway officer gave him another ticket. Doc's response to that was to tell the officer to just give him the damn book cause he was not stopping again for anyone. The night in jail was not too bad but the hangover and the judge were both pretty rough on Doc the next day. He will be able to drive again in about 6 weeks.

MOTHER NATURE

Spring is the time for rain showers and thunderstorms. Sometimes these can be scary with the lightning zapping all around. But a gentle spring rain late at night when you are under the cover and the rain is pitter patting on a tin roof will put you into a deep and restful sleep. Even a thunderstorm can be good. The sound of rolling thunder, rumbling thru the air far off in the distance can be very nice. Ancient man feared the thunder and the lightning, but we here know that it is just part of spring and summer. I don't know anyone whose house has been hit by lightning or even anyone that has been hit but the loud clap can still frighten people. If one is at peace with oneself then the sound of thunder can be pleasant. You can relax in your warm dry and peaceful home safe and secure in oneself and with nature.

This is just one of the many wonderful experiences of living in the country. After the storm, the air is fresh and cool and Mother Nature has had a drink of water. The flowers bloom, the birds sing, and all is right with the world. Our fear of nature is uncalled for. Mother Nature is our friend.

EATING MELONS

Eating watermelon is an art. You don't eat watermelon with a knife or fork, you eat it with your hands and if your mouth does not get messy, you ain't eating right

First, the watermelon must be fresh from the fields, stolen is sweeter but if you must, then go buy one. Take the melon to a nearby stream and place it in the shallows of a shady spot and let the cool water trickle over it for a while. Don't ever place it in deep water, a heavy melon will float and go down the stream. When you think the melon is cool enough or your girl won't let you kiss her anymore, then get the melon out and slice it. Only cut the melon in half, not the dainty slices you see in stores. Watermelon should be eaten with only two things, your hands and your mouth. It will be messy and will run down your mouth and coat your chin but the taste is worth the mess. The good thing about a melon is that it will not stick with you. It is a natural sugar and so will pass.

In fact, you will be "Passing" quite often as the evening goes on. The only thing in the world that can compare with a stolen and cool sweet watermelon is the girl you share it with. Pick your partner carefully. You might have to go find another melon right soon.

SMOKEY AND THE HUMAN

This is a true story, the name is real and the event is real. Only the location is not known to you readers. I can tell you that it is not located in Coldbeans. We do not always choose our destiny and partners.

One day, Dave was leaving his home to go shopping. When he opened the door, there standing patiently waiting was a gray cat as if this was his home and just why did it take Dave so long to open the door? Anyway the cat, which would be named "Smokey" due to his color just walked in as if this was HIS place and he was glad that someone finally opened the door to his home. Dave went to the store, closing the door to the house that he thought was his but was soon to find out different. He bought the items he needed. He also bought a littler box, cat food and a nice basket with pillow for the new house "guest". Like all cats, Smokey was indifferent to this new person but did finally train him to learn to pet when wanted and the proper place to put HIS bed, which was not the one Dave bought, but the king size bed already in the house. Smokey was not a dumb cat. Some humans can be hard to teach, but Dave was easy to train and seemed to accept this new "person" as a permanent resident. All is well with them; they have survived two hurricanes and the training that Dave had to go thru to make a decent home for Smokey.

We do not always have the chance to choose our live in mate, but Smokey had chosen well and is very satisfied with his human pet.

A DEATH IN COLDBEANS

Aunt Mildred died early this morning. The funeral is for the end of the week. That is so all her 9 children can attend. They come from all over the country. Aunt Mildred lived and died in a plain wooden cabin. There was a potbelly stove for heat and only one light bulb to show her way around the Cabin. There were curtains on the windows, home made and an also an old sink with a bucket underneath to catch the water. The water came from a pump in the back yard. Aunt Mildred was 93.

The whole town is expecting a large crowd so there was help put up all the kin of Mildred. There were lots of happy adults, all with their children and their spouses. That makes for a lot of people to bed down. The town didn't care. If it had been ten times that many, the town would come to their aid. They are grateful to be able to help Mildred and her family at this time. There was one son, now a judge in Columbia, and two more were lawyers. Another son was a Baptist minister, two daughters successful in their own right and very happily married to successful men. There were two more sons, one an artist and another son, a musician for the college of arts in Charleston. Mildred never left home. The furthest away she got was about six miles to visit a friend. Mildred never had a car or a TV, but she had her own bible. That was her greatest treasure. It will be buried with her.

The funeral will not cost the family. It is a gift from the funeral home for all the time that Mildred gave to those suffering in pain. The cemetery donated the plot. The church paid for the flowers and three preachers asked to do the eulogy. It was the least they could do for a person who gave her all to her town and her church. She never asked for anything from anyone, but she is receiving all from everyone this day.

Now who was this woman who invoked so much respect, humility and generous from such a poor town? She was a dirt-poor woman whose husband died and left her with 9 children of various ages toraise. All of them graduated high school, 6 with honors. All of them worked their way through college and became successes in their own right. All of this because of the values she instilled in them. They learned about caring for those who could not help themselves. Their success was their mother's success. Mildred never knew the impact she made on the world through her children and the habits she taught them. The moral of this life is you never know the extent of your reach. Sometimes it far exceeds your own expectations.

UPDATES FROM THE EDITOR

This paper does not normally print ads; especially for cars but we know the owner and the car and it is a great buy.

The car is a 1956 Oldsmobile owned by Pete Radovitch, a long time resident here. It only has 50 thousand miles on it and has had the oil changed four times in it's life. It has the original tires and paint job. It is in good condition except that Pete can't find the top for the trunk. He took it off to haul cordwood and just never put it back on and now it is lost. Anyway, it is for sale and we expect a large turn out to look at Pete's car. Oh, to be truthful the upholstery is a little bit worn because Pete let his hunting dogs sleep in the car when it rained.

Also, the new burger king asked me to please ask the folks who constantly walk up to the drive up window and order, to please come inside. They are thinking of closing the drive up window, cause of lack of cars in our little town.

We are glad to announce that our friend Demetree Terrazzo is popular with the neighbors now that we know the soviets are not our enemies. We are glad because we like Demetree. He is a nice guy even if he does talk funny. The editor wants everyone to know that his Grandsons are now in the third grade, Jessie only took two years to get promoted, and Jon was a little slower.

WHAT TO DO WITH THE UN

Even to us clodhoppers here in the small town of Coldbeans the solution to that problem is easy. We are talking about the Un-united Nations and their lack of support in Iraq and helping to free the oppressed. Since the UN is located in New York and is such a pain in the butt just tell them that their lease is up and get the moving vans and go to France, a country that will love them and will never kick them out since the French will not fight for any cause at all.

The only question left is what to do with the empty building that is now called the "tower of babble". We could turn it into a home for the homeless or since no intelligence has ever come out of there, we could make it home of the Democratic Party and I even have a name for the building, "the Dan Rather home for democrats". And you thought we were stupid hicks

BACK IN TIME

Time travel is possible, you can not go forward and see the future but you can visit the past, as far back as you want and for as long as you want. I go back in time with each Coldbeans I write, it is part of my youth and although some of it is made up but lots of it is based on true events. I just saw Gene Autry on TV, with Pat Butrum and all of the horses and bad guys and at the end of the TV show, even an announcement to see Gene's feature length movie coming to your local theater. The bad guys wore black hats and the good guys did not kiss women. There were no Arabs, no terrorist, no cussing, and no nudity but still I enjoyed the show. Bye the way, the good guys won even though Pat helped in the rescue.

It is sad that America has changed and we now view things that were not even talked about in private much less viewed with family and friends in a Theater or on TV. America is moving backwards into moral decay. I prefer the values of the simple life in Coldbeans and that is why I write about it. Kids play here and have fun. They are not threatening by perverts or evil. Life was simple, you worked, and the fruits of your work gave you the life style that satisfied you. The government did not support you and the government did not tell you how to live and what to learn in school. Yes the good old days of yesteryear are gone, but I for one wish they were back again.

A VISIT TO THE FUTURE

We have talked about the time machine only working going back in time and that is just a mental pursuit but what if we could go to the future you live in now and see things from the eyes of someone over from 50 years ago. Would you be proud of your future and think they would like the way you live now?

There would be fast cars of a design and colors we could not have dreamed of in our time. There would be buildings that reach to the skies and highways that were wider than we could ever have dreamed. We could look at the great flying machines and all the wonders of things that did not exist in our time. If we visited a school, we would not be allowed on the school grounds, "protection" for the kids' safety you know. We would see kids with their cuffs dragging the ground and ill-fitting clothes and wonder what mother let her kid go to school looking like that. We would see kids with pins in their ears and nose and lips and even in their naval.

We would hear language coming out of the mouths of kids that we would not even have said in male company but being uttered around other kids and them not even batting an eye or being offended. Somewhere, in the time between then and now, the parents must had let down on their jobs and allowed the kids to develop these awful habits. We would see a future where we live in a fear of being bombed or attacked at any time, at home at work even traveling.

Now it is the sad truth that that awful future is our real present and we live in it. We created this future by not caring enough to protect our life styles. Knowing this, would we have wanted our kids to have to live in these conditions? Please, tell me what happened?

APPLE PEELING TIME

With spring planting out of the way the town turns to ways to entertain. One of the continuous arguments is that the only road thru town starts at one end and goes thru town and out the other side. The question is on which side does it enter and which one does it exit? See we have lots to do here! Why is church on Sunday? If church was not on Sunday then would we have to take a bath on Saturday night? Of course, church has to be someday so let it be a day when we are working in the fields. The women can go and listen to their own voices singing and we can plant in peace. We would still have to bathe one day of each week but no plan is perfect.

Now and then we can just sit around and do the things that are important like tell each other where the coons and possums hide, where the bees are building a nest and the apple-peeling contest. WHAT? You have never heard of an apple- peeling contest! Shucks, every small town in America that has apples has an apple- peeling contest. The rules are simple, first you peel an apple (choose carefully) and keep peeling until the apple is done or the peel breaks or is cut. The one with the longest peel from a single apple wins. He also gets to sample the pies made from the peeled apples. Those women must be pretty smart to get us to do the peeling thinking we are having fun and all the time it is a chore they wanted us to do anyway. Life is simple in the country but life is not boring

ARE WE SO DIFFERENT?

It seems strange to me that our little town would interest anyone. We don't feel like we are different from other people. We are aware that we lack the charm and grace of people living in large cities. We would not be happy there and don't think you would be happy with us living next to you. To those of us who have visited or lived in the "big" cities, life is different. Here we do not need locks on our doors and many times when it is hot, we sleep with just the screen door closed. Are we too trusting? Well we know all our neighbors, and their children and all of their kin. Now to be truthful we still are a bit careful of strangers around here.

Big cities have a lot of people going in so many ways, all in a big rush. If they did like us and walked maybe they would not be so uptight. We believe that it is not where you are going or how long it takes to get there, but what you did at the place you just left. If your children run off somewhere and you don't know where they are do you panic? Here we just wait until sundown and the kid comes home, well fed by a neighbor and happy to be out and about and was probably fishing or skipping rocks in the creek or catching fireflies.

The world here is safe and wide and to a kid, endless trails of wonder. In the big city, you must go to a park to enjoy nature; here it is all around you. Every farmhouse has a big tree with a picnic table under it and a tire swing hanging from a limb. On cool nights, that is where supper is served. After supper, we don't run off to watch TV but sit around and tell stories about the day or some account of the past that everyone wants to hear again and again. Now life is not all cake and ice cream here. We all have our problems, mostly money but sometimes a small family problem. We do not have the stress of living packed in close to each other. There is lots of land and fresh air between neighbors around here.

THE SOUTH AIN'T THE SOUTH ANYMORE

Once you could sit in the cool of the evening on your front porch, in your rocking chair and listen to the radio that set in the window and pass the time talking with your neighbor. You had your beer if you were male and ice tea if you were not male. It was quiet, no loud radios in cars zooming up and down the streets, no wild kids on dope. The air was good after a hot day and the evening breeze was cool and sweet. The lilacs blooming outside the house smelled very sweet.

Sometimes the neighbors would join in and if they came to your porch, you served tea with ice or, to the men a beer. If you went to their house, they served you. That was southern hospitality

There were no drunks, no loud boom boxes, no hotrods with broken mufflers and no ruffians to think they were the smart ones and the old people were the dumb ones. Well time would take care of that. WWII was over and America was proud, and respected around the world. There was only radio, no TV yet except maybe one in the hardware store window and then the picture was lousy. People had respect for the fair sex. Men did not swear in front of the women and women did not talk of sex in the open.

Kids were obedient and polite. They went to school to learn and someday have a family and a good job. They took their lunch with them; there was no money for fancy school lunches. They, for the most part spoke English and those that were new to this country, wanted to learn English, the language of their "new" home.

People did not live on government support. They chose to work. For those that could not work, the family helped with the care and the church helped. There were no food stamps and no welfare. If you were poor (and a lot of us were) you hoped that someday be rich. You did not blame the government for your being poor, because a lot of your friends were poor also. They had no money but lots of pride. You paid taxes, and there were not as many taxes back then.

America was a proud country and Americans were a proud people. America was respected around the world and all wanted to come to this country to live. The more that the government helps this country, the worse we get. Please stop helping us out; we will do well on our own, we have proved that in the past.

FIGHTING AND DRINKING

We are all comfortable in our hometowns where we went to school and the classmates we hung out with and the places that are familiar to us. Include in that are the memories that we gather as we turn into adults and make our way, sometimes in different locations. So goes Coldbeans.

Many who grew up here leave here but some stay and some return after a while. Just like the big cities we have our troubles also. One thing we very seldom have is drunk driving. No matter how drunk the individual gets his horse knows where the stable is and sometimes the rider sleeps in the barn with his horse. Of course after a while, the wife knows where he is and lets him sleep and the next day is worse on his ears than it is on his head. "Get a bath" "you smell" "go to work". Is it really worth drinking I ask you? Also like many other places we have a few drunks who like to get into a fight. This normally happens down at the general store and out on the street so as not to break anything. Money is very important after all because it can buy more beer. Generally when there is a fight and the sheriff has to get out of bed and come settle the argument he is not happy and the two people spend the night in jail.

Staying in jail with a hangover and meeting the judge the next day and knowing that your wife is also waiting does not give one a reason to wake up the next morning. Now if the sheriff does not get called and the crowd breaks up the fight, then they put their arm around each other and go back in the general store and drink some more. It does not matter to the horse, he know where he will be in a few hours. All in all, Coldbeans is like most small towns, not much going on, no murders, no shooting and very little cheating on the wife. It's just another day here

BERTHA GETS A TV

There ain't much happening in this quiet little place stuck away from the main highways and bye ways of our little ole state. Bout the only thing exciting is that Bertha bought herself one of those TV's and it took two men to haul it to her house and then she found out she need electricity to run the damn thing. That cost her more than the set cost. It is pretty though, with its big ole black and white picture staring back at you just like in the picture show, and there it is right there in the home.

Bertha got a little worried that anything you can see also can see you back, so when she is not dressed and watching it she has a big ole cloth a hanging over it. I don't know anyone who would want to see her dressed or undressed. She is kin though, my mama's aunt and half sister. Several homes here now have electricity, I t might be the way of the future. One of them, Bubba Lardbucket even has a light in the outhouse.

Some people are upset about the upcoming election. They mostly want to know why we need to change presidents so often. They are happy with the one we got; he doesn't bother anyone and never comes around with his hand out and that is all that counts.

More and more people are going to the Carolina Fried Chitlins on the weekend. This is the first fast food place to give us southerners what we like That Dorothy gal was back in town and wanted to know if she could organize some kind of reunion here Well anything with the word union in it is not looked on too kindly around here. She said it would be a group of her friends from allover and they would party and just have fun. She was told no way, we don't cater to no weird sex and drinking here except with kinfolks

CAT TEST

A special bulletin issued by the Coldbeans main campus of the University of Coldbeans in South Carolina has found after exhaustive research that blond cats born in the South are much smarter than the same breed of cat born in the north. Professor Elroy Muckenfuss of the Animal science lab and Campus cafeteria dept has found that cats born in the south react much faster to stimuli than cats born elsewhere in the country. Test with live rats proved this to be a fact.

A test was run on a northern and a southern cat of the same breed to see which one caught the rat in the room. The northern cat went after the rat every time while the southern cat just sat there and wondered how such a disgusting rodent could get in the room anyway and why did not some one come and kill it. The northern cat caught the animal and killed it and the southern cat threw up. This test proves the superior analytical ability of the southern cat and its proper upbringing.

We would like to welcome all those Florida people trying to escape that Yankee paradise called Florida. You are welcome. Please spend money while you are here

HARVEY

Harvey Muffinfuss moved to Coldbeans from upstate somewhere. He went around buying up old furniture, all stuff we were glad to get rid of. Then he called them Antiques and the tourist paid a lot of money for them. The more beat up the more antique he calls them and the higher the price. Ain't America great!

Harvey is single and not bad looking. Being as he is a storeowner (meaning rich folks to us) he is a good catch for some gal locally maybe. Only problem is that Harvey has very good eyesight. This makes him a hard catch for the type of plowing and spitting gals he has to choose from. After all, beat up furniture might make a good sale to tourist but beat up and mud ugly women are hard to give away.

When Harvey turned down the "cream of the crop" girls from around here, the men folks started raising their prices on their old stuff. Harvey moved his home and store to Too-kee-do and is doing quite well and from what we hear will be married soon to a rich widow. Well, as the saying goes, "when you paint an ugly barn, it is still just an ugly barn"

HOW TO RUN A SMALL TOWN

Coldbeans is preparing for its semi-annual wash Clem celebration. This happens only twice a year and is a big event around here. People start making lye soap months before the big event and everyone turns out to watch (from a distance of course). That is why Mrs.Carisha is washing him. She has no sense of smell. When he gets to stink too much for the house and it is springtime, everyone knows that it is Clem washing time.

The town went out and bought an old claw foot bathtub and put it in the yard. They started cutting wood for the fire to heat the water (Clem don't like cold water) In fact he don't like any kind of water. Once he got out of the tub and took off to the woods with his dog and the people a chasing him. They caught him in a briar patch and he was glad to get back to that tub.

We here at Coldbeans is pretty much laid back and don't let much of the real world bother us. That is why Coldbeans votes every election and every one votes. They may not all vote the same but they do vote cause it is one of the ways to let our opinions be known to those Washington peoples Once every four years we have someone come around and promise us everything we want and then he leaves and we quickly forget what he said. It is the only way to run a country.

COLDBEANS, A CHRISTMAS STORY

This story is really a Christmas story but I'm telling it now.

There was a couple that lived in the big city Columbia, the capital of the state. They lived in an apartment and wanted their own house. The couple was only recently married and the wife brought two daughters, young (about 6 and 8) into the marriage. The wife's father had about

50 acres up in the country, in a small rural area called pine Creek. He let them have about 5 acres to build on. They started out with a modest house and added on a basement. The house eventually cost them more than they planed and it put them into a bind. Christmas was coming and it was to be the first Christmas in a new home.

The couple talked about just buying gifts for the kids and nothing for each other, they agreed. Come Christmas morning the kids were excited and hurried down stairs to see what Santa had brought. The couple were there waiting to see their bright eyes and excitement at the presents they bought.

The first gift picked up by the children was taken to the father. It was a small-decorated bag with a ribbon on it. It said, "Merry Christmas Daddy". Well he got mad. It had been planned that the adults both not buy anything for each other. Hi wife let him rave for a while and then quietly said, "now that you are through making an ass of yourself open the bag." Inside the bag was a small piece of paper, a receipt from Bethesda, home for boys in Savannah, Ga. It was for a $25.00 donation, in his name to the orphanage he had once lived and it was for any boy who showed art talent, to be donated in his name. It was the greatest present he had ever received for Christmas in his life. He tried not to cry but the feeling was too strong. He broke down and sobbed. Sometimes, what you give has a greater reach than the mere cost of the item.

Bart Tarpacker got the idea to investigate the regulars in his jail and found that several of them only got drunk on Friday night for the quiet in the jail and some wanted the hospitality for the whole weekend. Now a jail is for wrong doers, but when you do wrong just to get in jail, it loses it value as punishment. Tarpacker talked it over with the mayor and they came up with a great idea. If you were a guest in the jail for three weekends in a row, then you were awarded the pleasure of working for the city for a period of one month doing the chores that no one else wanted to do like cleaning streets, picking up litter and maybe cleaning up the park. Being in jail is bad but having to work and be seen working is pure torture. This kind of cleaned out a lot of the guests in the jail. Of course the regular Friday and Saturday night poker game and drinking was still held in the jail, just you had to go home after it was over.

BRAGGING RIGHTS

A study has found that women prefer southern men to men from anywhere else. The reason for this decision is not too strange. Women prefer to have a husband with a large belly from drinking too much beer and unshaved and most of the time un-washed. This type of husband gives the wife an upper hand at the meeting with other wives when comparing the absolutely worst husband alive. In other words, it gives them the bragging rights or in this case moaning rights.

It helps if the husband can not wash dishes because he is watching the football game or has his buddies over to the house (unannounced) because they can't smoke their cigars at their own home "so come on over here and we will burn up a few" It is also helpful if the guys like to play poker and drink beer and laugh so loud that the poor wife can't sleep. It is also good if the men can't find the ashtrays that were set out in the middle of the table. Southern men excel at all of these traits. The fat tummy scratching, the belching and of course, the passing of gas, All of which means you have to call attention to the action. Wives of southern men choose their husbands carefully for the very purpose of bragging rights. Pity the poor man who can cook and iron and helps make the bed and take a bath every day. In the first place, this gives the wife nothing to complain about and worse than that; the other wives will not believe her anyway, The proudest wife is one whose husband is out of work and then she gets to play the full horror of living with him. All of the women in Coldbeans love their husbands and are proud of them (all that is except for Caleb) and no one in Coldbeans likes him, not even his mother.

ADS AND INTELLIGENCE

NASCAR with all its advertisements on the racecars is the fastest billboard in the corporate world. All these sponsors pay good money and who can read them as they go speeding around the tracks? People don't watch races to see all these names on the cars, but in hope that there will be a crash and make this boring sport interesting. Maybe we should sew emblems on the baseball shirts of the ball players. At least ball games are brought to you by only one sponsor or at lest only a few. Nothing happens in this country without a sponsor. Sports, Debates, News, and every TV show ever made. Maybe we should rent out space in the schools for ads. That would bring in money. No, come to think of it, that would not be a good idea because then the kids would have to read and we know they don't like to do that.

If the kids won't read then they can't read the ads in the paper. Note that newspaper circulation is way down. Only ads keep it afloat. America is in trouble. Some kid in school today just might be our future president. The new oath, "hey dude, I be yo new president", cool huh? And you wonder why companies are sending their business overseas. Wake up America and demand your moneys worth from our education system. Hmm maybe the answer is that smart people might not vote the way you want, so keep the system dumb and control the country. Egad, that makes SENSE!

DIVORCE IN COLDBEANS

Essie May caught her husband, Elmer (once again) at the Hot House dance saloon. She caught him red handed. He was caught dancing with one of the girls and trying to make a "spend the night" deal. Someone called the doctor so he could be at the poor guy's place when she got him home. He was not hurt, she never hurts him when he is drunk, he can't feel anything then. She was waiting for him to sober up so she could whip the tar out of him. She never wanted to divorce him, that would make him happy and besides, she enjoyed making his life a reign of terror. He drank because she was mean and she was mean cause he drank!

Essie was not a sweet woman and few understand why he married her, except maybe he could not find a sane woman that would say yes. Marriage and divorce is the same all over, there are slight differences in the city and the towns. Small towns like Coldbeans seem to have fewer divorces but beneath the surface there are more unhappy marriages. In a large city divorce is so common that it is hardly noticed except for the wife, husband and children. A few neighbors may gossip and say quietly, "well I knew it would not last", also the bride's parents says "I told you it was wrong". Other than that it is commonplace.

This is not true in Coldbeans and being a small place everyone knows everyone and what they are doing and with whom they are doing it. There are no secrets. If a husband is a drunken lazy lout everyone knows and if the wife is a shrew mean, or does not keep a good house then all know that too. People in small towns stay together because they are in for the long haul and most try to work things out, change or just fool around on the other person. Sometimes, this solves the problem; because if caught, one or more can end up dead.

Marriages can be the right choice at the time that it occurs but many years down the road, people evolve or change. Taste and habits do not stay the same. No one is bad, mean or cheating, It is just that they can't stand each other anymore and the adult thing to do is part (as friends if possible). If there are kids, they will still be the kids of both parties, dad will be dad and mom will still be mom. The roles will not change, just the location where they live.

Around Coldbeans, it is not uncommon for the husband to just build another house on the same property and live near by. Family is important to the people here. Being it is his own house; he can drink, and smoke, walk around naked and scratches his butt when he wants. Sometimes, this life style gets old and the two end back up with each other, both aware that two people jointly become one couple united. This is the good ending. The flip side is one of anger, fighting, getting drunk and landing in jail. This is then a marriage that will not be anymore. Both parties are better off not seeing each other. Sometimes, the dumb people of the small town are not that dumb after all.

COMING HOME AGAIN

Normally when you leave home for a while and return, things have changed, but not in Coldbeans. Things don't change around here. This town is locked in a time warp, one of those times known as the "good old days" before 9-11 and drugs and parents not doing their jobs with their children. You walk down Only St, (It's the only street with stores on it,) so it is the "main" street. In truth it isn't a blvd either. All the stores that were here when I lived here are still here. Shakey is still trying to cut hair without cutting the customer but that old demon rum stuff is making that hard to do, and of course the benefactor of all Shakey's "accidents" is his brother, the Doctor, who works upstairs. This is why even though Shakey does not make much cutting hair; his brother pays the rent so Shakey can supply his brother with walk in business all the time.

The little schoolhouse that is wisely located far from the work a day life of the town is fast out growing its one room. Soon they will need a larger school and two teachers. Right now they are getting a bargain, one teacher for four grades. Of course it isn't that hard since some of the students spend years in the same corner before getting promoted. The consensus here is that when the student becomes smarter than his parents it's time to graduate and go into the business of plowing or hog farming. The smarter ones go into the moonshine business but the sheriff frowns on that since it cuts into his sideline of work.

Living in Coldbeans may not make you rich but it does give you peace of mind. There is no rush hour for work. No stress of hurrying to and from lunch (you eat it in the field). There is no traffic, no cell phones and just a calm way of thinking. The thought of the day is always "don't worry" and that "everything will work out" when it is ready. They don't sell many stress tabs at the drug store and yes the drug store does have a coke fountain and stools to sit on with your date and have an ice-cream soda. Too bad there are not many cute girls here, but the boys are no catch either.

DEATH OF A SMALL TOWN

Evolution is a fact of nature and society, People evolve, nature changes. Nothing can remain static. That is why this newspaper exists. Towns, like people, change. They grow and the families that once lived there grow up and others move in to enjoy the small town life. The thing that attracts people to a small town is the very thing that kills the small town. Coldbeans can only exist in our memories as it is a way of life that exists only in very few places anymore. In our minds it can continue to live, unchanged and a treasure of the past.

First, the families grow and there must be more homes. Not all can live on a farm so some come into town and create businesses. They enter the trade called "barter' the exchange of materials for money. It happens everywhere and money becomes more important than any other goal. Factories are built to make the items to sell cheaper than the tradesman skills can make them, and they lose their individualism. Then the final deathblow of a small town, enter a Wal-Mart or K-mart and the town suddenly becomes dependant on money more that skills. Skills die out and what was an ordinary item in the house becomes an antique of the past. Memories die and people laugh at "the old ways" of doing things. Pride in workmanship dies. The reasons for making something a certain way is lost and a treasure house of knowledge is lost for all time. Just like an endangered animal or plant, the small towns of America need to be protected or they will only exist in our minds such as these Coldbeans stories do. Man is his own worse enemy. As we grow, we destroy our own heritage. Can you imagine Coldbeans as the next New York?

CUSSING

Cussing is not what it once was, it was a male thing and never done in mixed company or around kids. Sure, you can hear a cuss word sometimes around here but that is when someone hits his finger with a hammer. Turn on the TV and you can hear language that would have been a disgrace years ago. Our kids, young kids, curse worse than any male did and worse than some males do now. Is TV following the trend or setting the trend?

I would hope (and I know it is stupid to hope) but can National TV clean up its language to help the human race, improve on it rather than to slide further down to the level of animals? Come to think of it animals don't cuss. The language tolerated in schools would not be acceptable in front of their parents, but schools are controlled by the guvmint and it might "harm" some kid to discipline him. I guess we need to tax the rich more so that we will have the money to feed the stupid and unwashed.

It is a shame that the rest of the country lives like that, but please don't come here, the bad language will only follow you.

DUMB CITY FOLKS

You know Coldbeans is not such a stupid place, sure we do brag about how dumb some of our people are but it is all in fun. Heck, the big city can outdo us easy and it is not because there are more people there, it is because some of the people in the big city are far more stupid than we are or else they would move to the country. They live in tall building, have to take a elevator to get to their floor and in an emergency, the elevator does not work and they have to walk down a lot of stairs. You would think that people living in those places would look down on the poor folks. Well there are people looking down on the people looking down on us.

Rule one: there is always someone smarter than you
Rule two: there is usually someone dumber than you
Rule three: we all hope that rule two applies more often that rule one.

Being stupid is no big deal in this world, there are lots of us. Just look around after each election and try to guess who the dumb ones were that voted for the idiot that won!
Being smart isn't easy either, you only have a few friends and most of those think you are a snob. Most of your friends are insufferable and owe you money. We might be dumb out in the sticks but we go home happy and don't have to live upstairs.

FAMILY PROBLEMS

Now and then something happens in Coldbeans that make it newsworthy. So goes the tale of Ellensue and her cousin, Earl Lee. It seems that they were lovers and got caught by Earl's Dad. He hit the roof and he hit it harder after he found out Ellensue was pregnant. The whole family (both sides) had a meeting and talked over the Idea of Ellensue and Earl getting married. The one problem was they were first cousins. Uncle Luke (on earl's side of the family) thought that it was not a good idea for cousins to marry. Uncle George on the Ellensue side of the family thought it was a good idea since it was his niece who was "knocked up" as he put it. The family arrived at the wise (?) decision that since they were already kin twent no reason for them to marry. I wonder if the baby will be as wise as his parents.

GRADUATION DAY

This was graduation week in Coldbeans. Now I know that elsewhere, June is graduation time but here it is in August because our kids learn slower than the big city kids.

The kids love graduation even though some of them will be back in the same grade the next term. Graduation means that the kid's family will be together and they will get to meet some of their relatives that they have not met before or at least seen in a long time. Little Mickey was the proudest of the kids, his dad came with a big policeman who seemed to like Mickey's dad cause he stayed real close to him. Mickey's dad lives a long ways off and will be gone for at least eight more years. Roland's family was the biggest. There was his mother, his dad, his mother's latest husband and two of her former boyfriends and his dad's present wife and several of his half brothers and sisters. There were also some kids that Roland was not sure if they were kin or not.

The kids who got promoted were proud but some of the kids who did not get promoted were very relieved that they would not have to learn new things but could stay in their present class again and the real lucky ones could now be in classes with their younger brothers and sisters. Education here is mandatory as it is in the whole state but the teachers don't worry too much about what the kids learn. It is keeping them in one place for a certain period of time each day that counts. The real learning comes when the kids get home and have to work in the fields or around the house. They have their chores on the farm and picking peas, milking the cows and raking leaves has more meaning than some of that history stuff and the math that is hard to understand.

Now you understand the country a bit better, you see that out here priorities count a bit different from the big city. Coldbeans quit taking graduation pictures several years ago. It seems that all the pictures had some dumb kids with the V sign made of two fingers and behind another kid's head. Sometimes they only used one finger and that somehow ruins the picture from being a keepsake. Too bad though, some day we may have some kid grow up and be smart and become an editor of a paper and be famous.

INTELLIGENCE

Do not confuse intelligence with being smart, we have people here that are very smart but even though they can't read or write they can think very intelligently. The reason for this thought is that Prof (higgie) Higginbottom from the SC institute for the insane, known officially as the state capital came to visit our little town. Now Higgie is very smart but he could not describe a pencil if you asked him. He could tell you the inter workings of the atom but a common pencil would take him about an hour to describe. Book learning is knowledge but common sense is intelligence. The ability to know when to get off the road cause traffic is coming is wisdom from experience. Knowing how far the truck will throw you when it hits you is intelligence. Some of our people have not been beyond the 5th grade but are very smart. I ain't seen a smart person from the big city yet.

Smart is not just in the knowing, smart is DOING. You can have all the knowledge in the world but it ain't worth a damn if it can't be put to use. We know what kind of tree to cut for use as railing, and a different kind for lumber. We know when to plow the fields and what the soil needs. This is wisdom learned from experience and handed down from generation to generation Book learning is nice and is needed to succeed in this world but smarts without brains is like a plow without a mule.

MEET JACK SPRATT

Now Mr. Sprat may not be the best fellow in Coldbeans to meet but he is interesting. Not many visit Sprat on his hog farm. Hog farms can smell a bit but Sprat's odor is worse. Sprat is our best marksman but he would never enter any contest. Mainly being that the rules of the contest demands sober marksmen. "Streak of lean doesn't" have any idea the last time he was sober or had a bath.

He is fortunate to have a wife with poor smell and even poorer taste. She makes all the shine he drinks and the hogs get all the leaving from the brew. This gives the hogs a bit of a hangover and they lay around all day just oinking. Sprat prefers to lie out there with them and as a fact his wife prefers that sprat lay out there too. Sprat sleeps and drinks and snores and drinks some more. Some times he will open one eye and see flies buzzing around the hogs and he will take his pistol and shoot a couple of the flies. The hogs don't even wake up. Sprat has never lost a hog or even nicked one yet. One stray bullet did kill a fly and whizzed by and caught Mrs. Sprat in the tush, nothing big was hurt but her hollering woke up sprat and he went to hollering also. This gave the hogs a meaner hangover, I don't recommend visiting Sprat or at least without advance notice and giving proof that you ain't no revenue man. He is the most interesting sight in Coldbeans that is alive and not moving.

By the way, Sprat doesn't eat fat or any part of his hogs. He sells them but does not eat food; nothing solid passes his lips that ain't homebrew

OUR RESIDENT GHOST

Every good southern town has a resident ghost. Here in Coldbeans m we have one too. Most ghost are helpful spirits that lend aid or advice to people and only show up when there is no one around but you, so if you relate this story the first thing people will do is sniff your breath for whiskey. Many are the tales of people lost at night on a strange road, suddenly there appears a kindly old man who tells them how to get to where they are going, and then when the hapless traveler turns around the person has disappeared. Well, we at Coldbeans are not to be outdone. We have our spirit also. No, I am not talking about the stuff that the sheriff cooks up in the jail for consumption but a ghost. Going way back to the horse and buggy days, (which is not that long ago here), there have been tales of a kindly old man that aids travelers when they are lost at night on a strange road.

Now of course, this is Coldbeans and nothing is normal here and neither is our ghost. Sure he gives "helpful" advices to lost people, but if you run across him please ignore the advice. The only reason that he appears way out on a lonely road at night is he is lost also. Sure, he will give you advice, but it you heed it, you will be more lost than before. If you are lost, the best thing to do is to find a farmhouse and ask to stay the night. Anyone will aid a traveler lost and will put him or her up for the night and welcome the company. You might even get breakfast the next day and you might be asked to stay over for a while and just enjoy the rural scene. By now, you should know that nothing is normal in Coldbeans.

VIDEO GAMES

There are no video games in Coldbeans. One reason is that to play one you need a TV set and electricity and those are two things that are not easy to find here. Sure they have the battery operated ones for kids to take to school to give them something to do while the rest of the kids are learning something but most of our kids are not smart enough to operate one. We here wonder why an adult would give a kid some money to go by one of those things so he can learn how to kill people. Kids here do not need electronic games to shoot at electronic targets. Most here have a rifle and before they can point it the first time, they are taught that it is a weapon and not a toy. Kids here also have BB guns but they don't go around killing birds and shooting at cats and dogs. That is cruel and a sign of sickness.

So the question is why do we allow the kids to have these things and why do we give them the money to go buy such a thing? Our first thought is, if a kid wanted something like that, he should go see a head doctor. Violence is a sickness. It is a sign that something is wrong in the head and should be looked into very carefully. It looks like that as a society we will have the most efficient killers in the world but ones who can't read or write. Now is that something to brag about, not here it ain't. Even in the military, where guns are a part of life, the soldiers are taught that a weapon is a dangerous thing and the soldiers are trained in safety. Teach your kid to read and write, not to kill.

Note to the readers" If at any time you feel you can identify with any of the characters in this book, seek professional help immediately!

WRITING

Writing is almost a lost art. People used to pride themselves on their handwriting skills. Now my handwriting looks like a drunken chicken walking across a piece of paper after stepping in a bottle of ink. If I wanted to send code to someone, and trust that no one could interpret what I passed on, all I would have to do is write it by hand. As the saying goes, I can read writing, but I can't read writing after it is written. It is a sad joke that penmanship is now out of style. In fact most things that do not take batteries are out of style now. The really bad thing is that we get all our information from the news on TV. The newspaper is almost out. I get it for the Sunday funnies only and the ads. Kids do not know the pleasure of sitting or lying under a tree and reading a book, a long book, and one that you hate to put down and go to school or work. The nice thing about books is that you can come back to the very point that you left the story or even go back and refresh yourself on the details. You can read at your own pace. The famous saying that "the person who does not read is no better off than the person who CAN NOT read" is very true. Please take up a book (this book for example) and read it. You will thank yourself afterwards.

WE ARE DIFFERENT

Coldbeans is only a jigsaw puzzle. Most young kids do not know what jigsaw puzzles are, although there are some in the hobby stores. Let me explain what I mean by jigsaw puzzle. Coldbeans as a town lives only in my mind; it is made up of many small towns across the south. No one town would fit this scenario; it could not be and thus it is mythical. Taken in parts a lot of the stories in Coldbeans are real people and events, somewhat embellished a bit but that is the choice of the author.

Coldbeans might have existed in some form at one time, but not as told here. All parts of these great United States we live in have wonderful stories and local legends. I was fortunate enough to be born and raised in the south so that is what I know and love and why my stories are southern. If I were born in Boston (God forbid) then I would find the north to be wonderful and the south a bunch of clods. It is all in your point of view. Stories can best be told with humor. People love to laugh and remember funny things, but facts are boring.

Sure, many here still have a well and some do not have electricity. It is available, but a lot of the south is still poor and has not caught up the lifestyles of urban living. Yet in parts of the south, there are great cities that rival the ones of the north. Just as big city folks would be uncomfortable here in the country, so would we be ill fit to survive in the city. Just as there is more than one flavor of ice cream, there are many life styles and each person chooses the style that is comfortable for them.

You city folks wear shoes around the house, to play and at work. You do not have the fun of going barefooted in the cool grass. There are times when we have to walk a dirt road in the summer, we would much rather have on shoes. The road gets mighty hot. Here, the rules are made by common sense, we don't need a rule to say, don't rob, or don't kill. We know that it is wrong.

Rules are made to tell the bad people what NOT TO do and good people already know this and do have not need a law to tell them what is good, but only to say what is bad. Look up the "thou shall" and the "thou shalt not in the good book and see how many of each there is. It is simple to enjoy life, just remember, if it harms another, don't do it. See, our simple logic beats the best legal minds in the country!

URBAN AND COUNTRY

I lived almost 30 years in Columbia, SC. I owned several homes and I have also lived in a high rise apartment building. I fought the traffic to and from work every day. I shopped in the malls and enjoyed the air-conditioning. The city life was a learning experience and thus I can see sides, the urban life and the rural life style. When I returned to my roots, the air smelled different, It took me awhile to understand that "this is what clean air is supposed to smells like." Walk on the unpaved roads, feel the dirt between your toes and smell the scent of the grass. Look up and see the clouds, not smog If you were not born in the country, it many not be the life for you but if this was your birthplace and where you grew up and all your friends live, it is HOME. If you were born in the city, you might find us a bit weird. How can we live without having a car or a suit and dress shoes?

We need big cities and we need to save our country way of life too. Both are true Americana. Do your part to save your way of life and preserve those memories for your children and their children. Our children should lead better lives, that is their legacy but the past should be there for them to remember.

Do not t forget, the mighty oak tree is only as strong as it's roots.

WELCOME VISITORS

Welcome back to Coldbeans. Come visit the little town that never was and never will be but should have been. Come enjoy our life style and maybe some day, you too will have memories of your past as are portrayed in this book and the previous one. We are in lower SC, location unknown to the state and also to many of the folks here. We do that to stay off the list that politicians use to come and torment the public and suck the money out of our pockets.

Coldbeans is down a small country road, unmarked with signs. Just look for a place that looks like progress missed it and the people are happy and friendly, and you are there. Sit awhile and chat with us. We will talk slow so you can understand us. Enjoy the town, but don't think of moving here, it is hard to get used to our lifestyle.

COLDBEANS SALOON RULES

There are a lot of reasons that Coldbeans is the ideal town to live in. If you move your family here then you might be one of the smartest families in the whole town. The fact that you did not have to move here counts as 3 minus points on intelligence. If you move here to hide from the law then you might already know some of our citizens. If you move here cause you are broke, out of work and have no skills then you might want to run for the mayor's job.

You can't just decide one day to move to Coldbeans. First off if you have kin here they you can leach off of them for awhile before you have to find a job. If your wife goes to work then that will give you time to look for a job and also get to know the residents of our town. If you by chance meet the mayor then shake his hand. No need to give him your name unless you are thinking of donating to his campaign for re-election. If you are single, male and have most of your teeth the other men might not like you but the women will.

We do have a few social rules to follow here.
Never date a woman older than your own mother.
Never turn down a free beer.

Never offer to buy a beer for a stranger who is already drunk

If you are married do not tell others. It is none of their business and they might be jealous of you.

Never offer to buy a round for the others at the bar if you are drunk. Some of the other people might drink two or three beers on your tab. The most important rule is never take your wife to the saloon. A female cramps the conversation and takes the focus off beer drinking which is why you should be there alone.

EVENING IN CAROLINA, SOUTHERN STYLE

Living in the south is not the way that many books describe it. We don't sit around strumming our banjos and singing "old black Joe" there are no black people singing as they come home from the fields. Life here is the same as for you city folks. We come home tired and hungry from working in the fields or where ever we work and wash up and eat supper. What we do, and you don't do, is after supper we sit on the porch and enjoy the world outside.

City folks come home, eat and watch TV. We watch Mother Nature. The squirrels are playing, the birds are getting ready for bed in their little nest and the night creatures are coming out to hunt. You can hear an owl hoot in the twilight, a train far off or just the normal sounds of nature changing from a day mode to the night mode. Sure, we country folks have no qualm with putting the old sofa on the porch, instead of throwing it away. It is good to sit on and watch the world go by. There are no loud car horns, no blaring of the neighbors TV, and no boom box from the neighbor's kids. Life is serene in the evening and that is the way it should be, Time to unwind and rest, put your mind at ease and enjoy the day that was and the day that will come.

So goes our evenings in Coldbeans SC

TOURISM PROBLEMS

Folks here in Coldbeans have been talking about all the curiosity lookers that are coming to this town because of the stories about us and how we live. Now we like visitors but we are not on exhibit. We welcome people, but all the cameras and the "gee ma, look at that one, ain't he stupid looking?" talk like that turns us off. We don't even mind the posing for pictures but hate it when they turn to their wife and say "this is one we got to send the kids, they will want to stay in school after seeing these photos"

In truth, we think that you sightseers are the stupid ones, and you have no manners either. We would not talk about you with you standing there, maybe after you leave but never in front of you. Oh well, take your pictures and spend your money and after you leave we will be the ones laughing. It is like being at the monkey cage at the zoo, who is the one who is laughing at whom, the monkey or the humans?

ON CUSSING AND SPITTING

In the town of Coldbeans spitting is ok but not on the street or in front of ladies. You can spit in Church, if you have your own bacca can and are sitting on the back row only. Cussing is only acceptable in front of other men, when you drop something on your foot or when the wife hits you for coming home drunk late at night. We do have standards of manners here. We are not heathens, or at least most of us ain't.

There are a few here; the banker is one who will be buried in an asbestos suit in a fireproof coffin. Above all other rules is that a gentleman (and here that means all sober males) must be polite in front of a woman other than his own wife. Every place must have rules and we have ours and they might be a bit different from your town, but we like or town and our rules.

VISITORS MANNERS

Yankees can be so rude, they come up to us when visiting and whisper "hey bubba, you know where I can get some hooch?"

First of all, I aint "bubba" and second, we don't make hooch, we do make moonshine, and it is for our own consumption and not for sale to Yankees. If you don't know, that is illegal. We may dress funny for you tourist but we are not dumb. Another thing is the "hey maw, bring the kids and come stand by this hick so we can get a picture with him." "Well, golly gee willikers" "that sure would be nice of you, sur" If we ever did visit the big city and our kids acted like that then we would whip their butts right there in the middle of the street. Being polite is the first thing taught by our parents. The second thing is to ignore idiots or fools. If you are looking for a sideshow, go down the road a bit. If you are looking for real people living their real life and enjoying life, look around. There are a lot of us here.

Remember, to teach manners, you must know and use manners yourself. It works best by example. We say "sir" and "ma-am" to everyone, regardless of age. We are taught that from the time we could talk. Children are taught by example and sometimes we see parents that either never taught their kids, or set a bad example. America is loosing its respect, both for their country and each other. Respect is given freely and earned the hard way, by example. If we lose God and respect, what do we have here in this great country?

LEARNING IS A GOOD THING

In the good old horse and buggy days, you traveled only in daylight and there were no motels. Thus you went a short distance or knew someone along the way where you could stop and rest. There were also times that you could just knock on a door and the tenants would put you up for the night and welcome the company. These limits to travel meant that your world was small but today the whole world is available for seeing. You can drive farther, go faster, and have many places to stay. There is airline travel and road transportation available. The world has gotten smaller. As we visit more we also learn about others, and other way of thinking. Thus it is more than an adventure, it is a learning experience.

Family can now live further apart and still keep in touch. Yankees visiting the south get married and move down here, so also the southerner that moves to the north. All of this movement helps to give us better understand each other and different ways of doing things. Our world is smaller now and with TV it is even smaller, we can see any thing on the earth and even to outer space and be right on our own chairs in our own home.

Yet with all of this we are still suspicious of our neighbor. We suspect another person because he or she is a different color or speak a different language. It is not the world that is small; it is our thinking that is not growing bigger.

Each new person you meet ads to your knowledge and each day that we find something new, is a day that we learned something and thus, we are a better person for that. Grow in knowledge and learn, but do not forget your origins or parents or where you were born.

CAT BURGLAR

Stealing is not common here in Coldbeans so when cats became missing most did not give it a second thought. Cats do roam and are predators. That is why we have them and they also serve as working pets. When cats at 6 different houses went missing, people began to worry that we had a cat burglars. Only cats were missing, no dogs. A lot of old ladies were worried that their "fluffy" was being used for dog food or some other horrible thing.

As editor, I put a mention in the Gazette about the missing cats and in no time at all, the problem was solved. A sweet little boy, name not mentioned, was kind enough to help a very lonely old lady by supplying her with "stray" cats to take care of and it made her feel good to be able to help animals and gave the boy two dollars for each "stray" that he rescued. The cats all were returned to their rightful owners a bit fatter and content but unharmed.

The little boy, who had no idea he was doing wrong was only helping the cats and the little old lady and by the way making a bit of change. He was not punished. It was explained to him that these cats had a home they liked and even though the little old lady was nice to them, they did miss their own home. The crime was solved and all is at peace here now.

YANKEES WELCOME

Be it north or south, we can all agree on a few things. Take for example, the state of Florida. We know that it is not part of the south, even though it is located below Georgia. Florida is an extension of NY, NJ, and most of those other frozen states. They all go visit Florida in the winter. Thus the famous title, "snow birds" so called because they migrate.

In some ways Florida is very much like the south. People can't understand each other. They never wear socks except for fancy dress. They hardly ever wear ties and suits. Most times, they are just laying about soaking up the sun, very much like here. Until our wives catch us loafing. The biggest similarity is that in Florida, the people are as hard to understand as the Yankees when they talk. That is, those that do speak a form of English but a lot don't. The nice thing about America is that you can go so many places and see so many different ways of living. New England, the west, the mid west, all are different.

We enjoy our lifestyle here and we hope that you enjoy yours. Lifestyles are like a bed, once you get used to it and it becomes comfortable, others beds seem to not be quite right. Good maybe but just not the same as home. We enjoy funning you Yankees about the dumb hicks of the south but in truth we enjoy you visiting and spending money here and going back home and talking about us. After all, we talk about you too. Y'all come on down here, and see why we are happy and we hope you will Be happy while you are here. Bye the way, we do welcome new residents

FAMILIAR SURROUNDINGS

Over the years we have had several of the men leave Coldbeans to find their fortune, most never returning to their birthplaces. Some return after they are dead to be buried at home but that is sad. You only come back when you can't appreciate the place? I am one of the few who left and went to the big world and finally when I got old came home again. I can talk about Coldbeans because I have seen both worlds. The real world that most of us live in and the world of Coldbeans, a place that many of us wish we could live in. If you were born here, then returning is a pleasant experience, but if you were born in the big city, then this place is very strange to you.

People and habits are different everywhere. Home life and the rules that you were taught are the main rules that you judge all other rules by. It is good to see other parts of the world and it would be good for some of you city folks to observe us and see our way of life. It is not for everyone. Only those blessed with a love of clean fresh air and freedom to spit and not hit anyone. Many of the things that you hate about the big city, you would miss after awhile here. It is like sleeping in a strange bed as a guest. It might feel good but it ain't your bed and is just not right. You may not be able to tell us want you feel is different but you know it is different.

FROM UGLY CAN COME BEAUTY

Sometimes in the middle of a manure pile, you can find the prettiest flower. Often, the brightest flowers require rich medium to grow in and not much is richer than a pile of manure. So too it can be with people from some families. Some of the sweetest people have come from horrible parents. Parents that fight and fuss drink and cuss all the time. It is like they set the example for what the child to not be like. Most children want to be like mommy or daddy but some parents are such a bad example that the kid thinks, "I will never be like them" There are times that setting a bad example can prove to the child what not to do, instead of the example to what to do. After all, men have married beautiful young sweet women, whose parents are as mean as a snake and ugly as a muddy road. They can only hope that blood does not always breed true.

NEVER GET MARRIED WHILE DRUNK

Poor old Jasbo had to go and marry a city woman. She was pretty and he was pretty drunk and they were both single so the next morning they both woke up married. Jasbo's new wife tried to make the best of the new marriage but there were a few little things on which she could not comprise. First thing right off she retrained Jasbo to hang the wash on lines inside the house. T'went no way she would allow strangers to see her undies hanging on the clothesline. It did not make any matter that Jasbo lived two miles back of sunset and no one but hunters came back that far, it was deemed that the cloths would be hung from lines in the house.

Now walking around a small house with clothes hanging everywhere is a might difficult. It got even harder when Jasbo would wake up with a hangover and need to go to the bathroom and find his hung over head with lots of panties and hose cling everywhere. It also did not help that his stumbling over all these clothes made his new wife mad and with that hangover her voice somehow seemed a bit louder and shriller. Shrieking does not help a hangover at all. The very short lived marriage was doomed to failure. It did cure Jasbo of marrying though.

ONE HAIR CLYDE

Clyde was a very suspicious person. After being burned by his ex wife in court and finding his girlfriend in hi his house cheating on him he became very careful Clyde lived alone after that and was happy to be alone. In fact because Clyde was a loner after all of that, he did not want company, had no phone and depended on no one. If he left his house to go to town, he would secretly place a hair from his head in the door jam before closing the door. When arriving home, he would check to see if the hair was still there. Clyde did not like people and frankly, people did not like Clyde. They were all happy with this arrangement. Even the busy bodies from the church refused to visit Clyde to try to get him to come to church.

It was rare for a single man to go unbothered by the single women in Coldbeans but no woman was that desperate for marriage and that statement tells volumes about the reputation of Clyde. Now, if you pull out a hair from you head every time you leave the house, you will with time grow bald and in Clyde's case he was going bald before he got this habit. When Clyde died, he had two hairs left so the timing was great for him. They had to pay the mourners to come to the funeral. Even the preacher had to be reminded of her duties to the dead. Clyde was buried on his own property and to be faithful to the end, a hair was inserted into the coffin before lowering into the grave. The location was left unmarked as per his wish

STRANGE EATING HABITS

Eating habits vary from area to area. We enjoy watching the Yankees try to understand how to eat something that is foreign to them but to us it is just home cooking. If you are southern and go to Boston don't just order tea. They will ask you "lemon or cream?" You look at them as if they are touched and say, "Iced, thank you." We drink tea with ice, this is the south and we are not in the cold north. Give a Yankee some grits and if he does not throw them at you he will start putting on milk and sugar. Hell, this is corn but not corn flakes fellow. Grits are just ground corn, not a strange vegetable. With grits, you use ONLY butter and salt and pepper. You can put a soft fried egg on it also if you like but bust the yellow.

Collards and turnips might be a bit harder to get used to. I am not sure I best tackle the southern term "pot licker" right now. We won't try to teach you how to eat possum or coon. I don't want to make you sick while reading this. Our diet came about back in the days when you lived off the land and had to make do with what you could catch or grow or steal. Almost nothing alive got past the cook pot but maybe snakes and skunks. Sometimes snake is good to eat but a skunk is never good, alive, or dead. Wherever you live, what ever you eat, it is because you have grown up with that diet and it is normal to you. After all we don't frown on the French for eating snails.

MORTGAGES

We don't have a lot of mortgages here in Coldbeans. The bank makes a few but being as we are poor most can't afford regular monthly payments and just live on family land. It does not take long after the kids are grown for them to build their own house so they can walk naked inside when they want. When they get married, times and demands change. The wife wants a few pretty things and a second outhouse just for herself. Then is when the banker makes his living. Mortgages here are only for 10 years or if the signer goes to jail and can't make payments. The reason for the ten year limit is that most men want to get away by that time to parts unknown and the bank doesn't want that ugly shack on family land to have to sell.

A few of the "homes" would be better set on fire and collect the insurance than to try to resell to someone outside the family. It has been known that sometimes, someone will buy the house and move it to their land cause it is cheaper than building one. If it is a well build house it can make it to the new location without falling apart. If not it is sold as firewood, you haul yourself. Most times the house last longer than the marriage.

RUB A DUB

Most of us men have gotten used to the idea we have to take a bath on Sunday morning for church but some women get downright obsessed with the idea of bathing. We would prefer to take the bath on Saturday night but that can kind of interfere with our drinking time. If we didn't have to heat the water I think women would bathe everyday. When I lived in the big city, I knew some women that took a bath morning and night. I guess they got dirty easy. I admit that being clean feels good but getting clean does not. All that scrubbing and heating the water is work and can turn you off to being clean. At least once a week, Coldbeans smells good and that is for Sunday Church. I think that is why church was invented, so man could clean his body for worship and his soul for redemption.

It is easier on the women to bathe because they do it sober but we men have to do it with a hangover. There should be time between Saturday nights and Sunday mornings to get your mind right before having to get wet. Oh well, a man's got to do what a man's got to do, but why does he have to do it every week?

CLEAR DIRECTIONS

Getting lost on a trip can be fun if you don't have to be somewhere important at a certain time. If you have time and gas, just slow down and enjoy the view, it will take you somewhere that people can tell you where you are and most of the time, how to get to where you are going.

The place you stop might be so interesting that you may want to explore the area and stop and meet the people and take some pictures. Most of us down here love to have our picture taken and when you get home you can play the game of "count the teeth in that ugly sucker" Country folks can tell you how to get to somewhere familiar, though not the most direct directions and sometimes not the clearest directions either. They will "splain" slowly and tell you the way they go from here to yonder. The directions might include landmarks that are not familiar or no longer exist but you are supposed to know what was there "bout" thirty years ago. For some reason, direction from where you are to someone's place is easier to remember than to a city or town. Be ready to go to "Uncle Eddie's" old place that burnt down a few years back and turn left, or to the "old oak tree that was once there on the corner and go right.

It is best to just not pay attention to directions and just enjoy the drive till you get to somewhere that is on your map. Meanwhile, you will see some things that city folks don't see like fields, meadows, cattle and pretty barns and silos. Getting lost can be educational and interesting and you might want to get lost more often. We here in Coldbeans are lost a lot according to people that know us.

HISTORY STARTS TODAY

Someday there will be more cars in Coldbeans than horses or mules. Someday, the town of Coldbeans will be a big city with stoplights and traffic problems. Someday, the town of Coldbeans will not be the quiet town we grew up in. At that time we will have lost sometime but will not know it then. Later on we will miss the place where we grew up and the way we grew up and call it the "good old days." Each generation has its "good old days, That time when they were kids, and life was simple and innocent. It is not the town that changes so much as it is us.. We see things from a different view; we are taller, hopefully smarter, and more mature. The halcyon days of youth are gone and the work a day world with weekends off is all we can look forward to. There is one thing that is not lost, our memories. but when we die, the things that were important to us die with us unless we record them so that the people of today can relive the "good times" that we had in days gone by that is not here for them. Each generation thinks that the world started with them and ends with their childhood. The world did not exist before them and changes as they grow up. Today is normal for kids of today, but yesterday was normal for us and tomorrow will be normal for the next generation.

It is our responsibility to preserve those memories that we found that was so important enough to remember and share them with the future. Try to sit with your kids and tell them about the wonderful world that you grew up in, they will be bored to death but later on, they will remember some of the things that you told them and thru that memory your past will continue to live. I have photos of people from my grandmothers past and I have no idea who they were but they were important enough for her to preserve in an album. Photos deteriorate with time, but new processes have evolved to save those treasures. We can save the photos, but we still don't know the history of those pictures. That part is lost to time. History is important, not right now, but for the future. Save as much as you can, sit and talk with your children. It is thru their eyes that history will continue to live

GOING TO CHURCH

We men all agree that two things are bad about having to go to church on Sunday, First is having to take a bath and the other one is once you are in church you have to stay awake or at least not snore. I can't fake the bath but as long as I don't snore I can fake the being awake. I like the preachers that just drone along is the same tone all the time. The ones that jump and shout keep me awake. If I have to stay awake through the whole service I am cranky and don't put money in the basket where it is passed.

If I am hung over bad, I can fake being awake by sleeping with my eyes open. Yes it can be done with enough practice and a lot of whiskey. Going to church drunk or hung over is not a nice thing according to the women. We agree but sometimes being drunk makes the sermon go down a bit better assuming that we even listen. The purpose of church is not to make you a better man, it is to keep the wife happy, and with that you can also be happy. Another reason is if no church, then no Sunday eats. That is the biggest reason for going. It sure ain't going to keep me from that place down under and my wife is always telling me that I am going there.

HAPPINESS

The rooster is a good alarm clock but he doesn't get you out of bed on a cold morning but you bet the wife does. She wants you to turn up the heat and get the stove going and make coffee while all she does is get the kids up for school. If that rooster was not a tough old bird, I might have him one Sunday for supper. A warm bed, a feather comforter, and a cold morning, all make you want to stay in bed. The chickens, the hogs, and the kids make sure that you don't stay in bed. Such is the life in the country.

The kitchen is the warmest spot in the house in the morning. Having to heat the water for a bath also helps to heat the kitchen a bit. Getting the kids into the tub is hard work but getting them out is harder. So goes the life of living in the country. Once you are up awake and had coffee you step out on the porch and smell the air and see the view and it all becomes worthwhile. You are viewing nature, fresh in the morning and you are not staring at someone's house, a busy street or nosey neighbors. If you have grown kids and they have a house near you they might stop by for coffee and to make sure you are ok. That is family. The dog is just coming out from under the house and stretches. His day has started too. The hens are busy doing their thing in the nest and the day waits.

There are no busses, no trains and no cars going back and forth. All is peaceful and right but not all morning can be like that though. Even a storm can be enjoyed from the comfort of a warm and safe house. That is the secret of happiness, Safe and warm, where ever you live and however you live.

VOTING TIME IN COLDBEANS

It is time to vote here and vote we do, be it for the president or just the local sheriff. We know that who we vote for means that is whom we can complain to and or about later on. All that can vote do vote. The voting booth is set up in the church and on that day it is not called the church but it is renamed the "Coldbeans polling place" thus "separation of church and state." We make sure not to pray while we are voting. Local elections turn out as expected. The guy in office now wins for the next term. That is because we trust the crook we know and not the new crook. We are lucky to seldom have any outside campaign speeches. Most politicians either can't finds the place or don't care about us anyway. Only the new ones running try to get our vote. Voting is a pain but we do it because it is the American way and that is important to us. After all would you want the guvmint to choose your politicians?

The best part of voting is right after you cast your vote; the sheriff is standing there with the ladle and a cup for the shine that he serves every election time. Never before you can vote, but right after have you voted you have a sip on the sheriff. If the Mayor did that, we might like him a bit. He is a tight wad with his own spending money. Ours he can spend easy.

Heck our politicians here are not different that all over the country, just that they are honest about being dishonest. That is what this country needs, more honest crooks in office. These dishonest ones are driving us to the poor house. It is the AMERICAN WAY to distrust your elected officials, it took many years for them to make us distrust them and now that we do know they are crooks we don't mind, at least they are honest about being dishonest.

NEW ENTERPRISE

We have a new enterprise here in Coldbeans. Sam, down at the general store is now stocking concrete blocks for those who have a car or truck that does not run, cant' be fixed or can't be sold. You can purchase them or rent them by the month. They are also useful for supporting the house or anything that you want off the ground. I wonder why we did not think of that. it is an idea that could catch on around the country. Sam got the idea from visiting his relatives in the big city. The wanted him there to see his new grandbaby. Also he got to see a picture of the daddy of the baby, who could not be there because he has 6 more months to do in jail.

I've got to get that boy's address; he might know some of the same people that I know. If you are wondering why the blocks instead of getting the car or truck fixed, well first the local garage closed up for lack of business and what he got did not pay him anyway. Second, why fix something that will just break down again? Retire the old thing and some day a Yankee will come by and offer good money for it thinking we don't know it is an "antique." We get rid of many tools and junk that way. One man's junk is another man's collectables.

ONLY ONE AMERICA

The War Between the States has gone by many names. It has been called "the recent unpleasantness": and "the war of northern aggression." It was the most violent war that Americans have been in. See the movie "Cold Mountain" and you will see just how vicious it was. Yankees think we in the south are still fighting the war. We here in the south are Americans just like the northern people, but we do have fun with you tourist about that incident. The south is cast as a bunch of dumb country hicks. We are glad to let you people think that. Southerners do not think the same way that the north does. I guess it is the upbringing and the life style.

We admit that we have fun with Yankees, but that is all it is just fun. Deep down, we are all the same people and are all proud of America, "Hick's", Dixie-crats", or country yokels, call us what you want. We love to have you come visit and spend those Yankee dollars. Visiting the south to a Yankee is like being in a foreign country and when we go north, it is the same way, yet we all share the same pride in our country. You know what, It ain't you and I, its those dang westerners, from places like California and Hollywood that we have to be careful of.

IGNORANCE AND STUPIDITY

Ignorance and stupidity are not the same thing, Ignorance is untrained, and stupidity is unable to learn. These limitations can be put to good use. After all, who has more experience at stupidity than the people here in Coldbeans? Stupid people for the most part are honest because they are not smart enough to know how to steal so stupid people would be great in congress. Can you imagine an honest but dumb congress!!! Ignorant people can be trained to do things. They don't have to be aware of what they are doing but they will do well whatever they are shown how to do. Let us put this untapped source of labor to work for us. We have had enough of the smart people stealing form the guvmint and from the people.

Wait a minute! That is what the new program in the public school is about. They are teaching the kids how to be dumb. Dog gone it, the guvmint beat us to that one.

COLDBEANS SCHOOL BUS

At a Coldbeans town hall meeting, it was discussed why we had no school busses. Harvey stood up and said that all our kids walk to the school since it ain't far to go. This was not acceptable by the school "bored" of education their "logic" is that if you have a school, you have to have at least one school bus to comply with the guvmint standards. Since we don't have a bus, the town was mandated to get one, no mention of where we would get the money to buy the bus. We hooked up a mule and wagon to transport the kids but this was not acceptable by the powers above so we had to find a way to get a school bus. We found one in the next town and it was not in use and for sale. We had to tow it home since the reason they were not using it was that it was broke down. Coldbeans now has a school bus. The fact that it has never seen the school is immaterial. We had to get one to comply and so we did, there twent nothing said about it running.

ONCE A MARINE

Tadd came home from the Marines. Tadd had retired with 20 years and had not been home but once a year since he enlisted. Tadd loved the marines and he retired because the commandant asked him to "for the good of the service." Tadd was what you might call a "zealot" He woke up as a Marine, he slept like a marine, and he ate and worked like a marine. If there was a poster boy for being "too much marine" Tadd's picture would be on it.

Tadd was home, not that he wanted to be and frankly a lot of people around here were not happy with Tadd being home. Tadd thought that civilians should all walk "in step" It was the "orderly" way to walk. There was no commissary at Coldbeans to buy his things. When the corps did a job on that boy, they did a good job.

In truth, although the corps would not admit it, Tadd was a bit too much marine for the Marines. He was too much for his family also and so the wife left him, He was left with the teenage boy and two young girls. We here were all betting on when the social services would be visiting his house for a workup. Now it is strange how things work out. Only a child could melt the heart of a rough and tough Marine. It was not too long and the kids had won and Tadd was a softie in their hands. He was playing ball with the boy and drinking tea from the little cups with the girls. All of this was done behind closed doors of course, after all Tadd had his pride. One day, the whole puzzle came together. There was a knock on the door and there was the kid's mother, with a sweet smile on her face. She smiled and Saluted and said "permission to enter sir" Of course no answer was needed. He could not answer her because there were tears in the eyes of that tough marine.

Love is stronger than any drill Sergeant. That dedicated marine changed his life and enlisted in the Husband and Father corps for life.

BAPTISM POOL

We had to clean the baptism pool out again. The preacher has got to quit submerging babies, they come up, and the water turns yellow.

We tried to convince her that sprinkling is just as good on infants. Also you can't do a good baptism if the candidate is drunk. He doesn't know his own name much less why he is doing what he is doing. The preacher thinks that the more "converts" she gets, the better job she is doing and the better that person will be. In truth, Baptism has not changed a single man from here. He still gets drunk, cusses, and spends a bit of time in the jail. If jail can't convert you, then a small pool with water will not make you sober. It does please the wife for a while though and that is the husband's purpose for the whole act.

Outside of baptism, drinking, and just a bit of fighting, there is not a lot to entertain people here. The only other time the men are happy to see the preacher gal is when she comes to visit, then the men know there will be good eating and the wife will be nice as sugar.

There is even a drawback to the preacher visiting; you have to take a bath, which is almost as bad as the baptism dunking. You are damned if you do and damned if you don't, so go figure a woman's thinking.

CIRCUIT COURT

We have a circuit judge come around about once a month to hear cases. He seldom gets any business here in Coldbeans. Most of the cases are drunks and they plead guilty to being bad to their wives and are sentenced to live with their wife for 3 months without getting drunk again. Now that is enough punishment for any drunk since most of them drink because of their wife. Since the judge can dispense with his cases in about an hour, that leaves 23 hours to sit around sip a few drinks and tell lies. The law is easy here in Coldbeans. If you don't hurt someone and you don't shoot someone's animal or damage their property, you can get off with a $10 fine and a drink with the judge. Keeping the peace between law enforcement and the court is done best with a few sips of the sheriff's home brew or more accurately, jail brew.

For real crime, like violence, we let the lady of the family handle that. Most husbands have to be drug home drunk. It is easier on them to face their wives that way instead of sitting in the jail, getting sober and then seeing their wives. Our women are not mean to anyone but their husbands. We have not figured out if the husbands are drunk because the wife is mean or she gets mean because they are drunk. Never in the history of Coldbeans has there been a woman arrested for husband beating. The husband knows where his bread is buttered so he ain't gonna tell. It is best when your favorite drunk is your friend the sheriff and he is the one that got you drunk. No woman has ever tried to beat up the sheriff yet.

CURING THE DRUNK DRIVER

Wives use a little trick when their husband takes the car or truck and goes to town to get drunk. This method is not used all the time and works best if only used occasionally. You see, when he is driving home drunk, he is familiar with the roads and so will not run off and go into a ditch or hit a tree. He has made the trip before. Before dark and after the husband and the car is gone, the wife and kids take a shovel and did a shallow trench across the driveway, not too deep, that would damage the car when he drives over it. Just enough so that when he thinks he is about home, relaxes thinking that he made it without a cop stopping him he can see the house, and speeds up just a bit. He is driving without lights on, so as to not alert his wife that he is late or he is drunk. If she knows he is coming, he is aware that there will be an angry wife behind the door with a fry pan in her hand and a good aim.

The poor husband is looking at the house to see if there are lights on or anyone awake, he knows his drive so he is not watching the road. When he hits the shallow ditch, the roof of the car stops his head from going to far. This kind of bump would scare anyone back to being sober. But it is not over. No wife would go to this much trouble and not be there to see it happen. This usually cures the wandering drunk for about a month or so. Men have short memories and it is bound to happen again. About three times is enough so that it is not necessary to repeat it. This will not work in the city or with a paved drive, so don't try it.

GET LOST AND ENJOY IT

It is hard to get lost in Coldbeans if you were born here. It is almost as hard to get lost if you are just visiting. Natives know every tree, squirrel, rabbit and trail between their house and town. If you are new or just visiting, you can stop anywhere you see someone and ask for whose home you want to get to. People are friendly and will after giving you directions, ask you to just stop for awhile and have a glass of tea before going on your way. We don't get a lot of new company, so we take every chance to get to know the new people.

It is hard to get lost in the town also. There is Only Street and two dirt lanes, one on each side behind the buildings. This is a simple place with simple people. Even if you got here accidentally, you will probably spend a bit of time here before you continue one to where you were going. There are a lot of towns like us around the area. We have more than palmetto bugs, Spanish moss, and country hicks here. Just stop and sit a spell and soak in the good life, slow living, and honest people. That is why South Carolina is called "friendly places, smiling faces"

LIFE OF A BABY

A baby is born, it does not ask to be, but out it comes into a new world. The baby can't do anything on it's own. The baby's world is its mother for a while and then life expands and the father is now part of the baby's world. At first, all the baby has to do is sleep and nurse. Then the nursing is removed and there is a new thing, a bottle, not as good as mommy but that is the only way to get nourishment now.

The bottle is removed and the baby now has to chew its food. Life is becoming more complicated. Then the nice tasty soft food is replace with more real food and more of a demand on the baby. Demands continue, the baby has to learn to be potty trained and to eat on its own. More demands, the baby must talk and walk, crawling is not fast enough now. In front of his life is school and learning to read and write, more pressure. Finally the baby is grown, and is a high school graduate.

He joins the military and is sent to war. War is the worse of the entire life events he has encountered, and survival is harder. The young man is in the wrong place at the wrong time and his short life ends. Why all the effort to learn and then to have all that experience wasted? Is life so cheap that it can it be wasted so easy? Why did it have to happen? There were bad people in the world and they thought they should be in charge of the world and killing meant nothing to them, only the power meant anything. And it was all done in the name of religion For this, an innocent life was lost and many more along with it. What a waste. Is life so cheap that we don't care about our children? War will never end, and many innocents will die. Mankind has not grown to understand the real reason for war. It is power over life. Remove greed and the lust for power and nothing will change, man is a predator and only the woman knows how it is to lose a part of her that was in her body. Can we do anything to stop this nonsense? Only when life is more important than power will we be able to stop some of this.

WONDERFUL OUTDOORS

A boy is the same all over the world, there is no school in the summer so they have no reason to get up or do anything. If school were in, they would have a thousand things they wanted to do rather than go to school. Summer is a carefree time, no books not teachers but all of a sudden mom can come up with chores like pick up your clothes, clean your room and help your father in the fields. What the heck is vacation for anyway?

There are things to do in summer; there are tall trees that have not yet been climbed to the top and time to catch crawdads in the creek or chase butterflies. Now, I ask you, can any kid resist playing in nature's playground? The only thing that kids do not have time for in the summer is chores. Summer is a time for exploring but if the kids knew that "exploring" was not play but learning, they might not be so enthusiastic about it. Kids learn things in school but the biggest school is the great outdoors. The outdoors makes itself interesting to a kid, he will stare at everything and wonder how it works, and thus he is learning.

This natural curiosity is the link that will help him in the adult world; it is a yearning to learn about things, why and how they work. The countryside is safer to play in than the big city, no hoodlums, no drugs, and no traffic. One of the first lessons we learn in the outdoors is about going barefooted. It is great in the cool grass and the cold water but not so much fun in a fire ant bed. We learn the most important lesson by making a mistake. Mistakes are seldom repeated. Life in the country is great, don't you wish you were a kid again and could explore the wide wonderful world?

COLDBEANS AIRPORT

Our airport only had one plane and no regular schedule anyway, so it is no big loss. The plane was an old crop duster that was not safe for dusting anymore and would hold the pilot and one passenger, drunk or sober but most passengers liked to be drunk while on the flight. The plane only flew to Too Kee Doo to connect with the big plane to Charleston and Columbia. In truth, you had to be dumb or drunk to take the trip. It was only 2 hours by horse and wagon, 3 hours by mule and 45 minutes if you took the car and the paved road. Not a lot of our people like to drive on the paved road, it is too smooth and they fall asleep which is kind of bad if you are doing the driving. Anyway, the airfield will be returned to its old use as an okra field. Anyone want to by a used hanger?

JACK AND SARA

Sara lived in the city when she met jack. They courted and got married and moved to Jack/s home, out in the country, near Coldbeans. Now Sara was a city gal and scared to death of being alone in the back woods at night. Meanwhile, Jack had to work late lots of nights and so got home a bit after dark. Sara would not know who was coming down the drive and so she would get scared and cream her head off. This bothered Jack and he bought her a gun, a pistol to keep her from feeling like someone could hurt her.

After repairing three bullet holes in the door of the car and replacing one windshield, jack figured out that Sara was a bit restless and the gun did not help. When Jack came home, he would be blinking the lights and playing the radio loud and honking his horn. This see med to work but it made Jack a bit nervous and the neighbors a bit angry at the noise of him coming home. Jack spent the money to have a large street light put up next to the mobile home and Sara could see better. From that time on the only time Sara shot at Jack was when he came home drunk and forgot to turn on the radio and lights.

RONNIE AND BESSIE

Bessie Mae just divorced her husband for the third time. When he is drunk, she can't stand him but when he is sober, she is in love. Bessie Mae's husband is drunk a lot of the time. Bessie does not mind the divorce, she has a standing order with the lawyer, and all it takes is a phone call to him. It would be easier to just kick Ronnie out of the house but Bessie is as mean as a snake on a hot road. Poor Ronnie had to pay the cost of the lawyer and the cost of the court each time, so she is slowly driving him broke. If he were not a good mechanic, he would have been broke a long time ago. Now, in truth, Ronnie has a reason to drink, it is called Bessie Mae. When sober Ronnie can't stand her and when drunk Ronnie gets divorced. It is a no win system. Ronnie can't feed himself when drunk and when he is sober he runs around with the women and that makes Bessie mad and she marries him to stop the running around. Now I know this does not make sense, but does anything that happens in Coldbeans make sense?

HIGH COST OF EDUCATION

School in Coldbeans is something that kids don't like and it is normal for kids to not like school. After all kids would rather be anywhere than having to sit and learn things that does not interest them in the least. Only one person hates school more than the kids and that is the teacher. It is hard to find an educated person to come to a town like Coldbeans to teach. Look carefully at the applicant and find out why he wants to teach in a small country town at a low salary and not in the big city at a much larger salary.

Here you have the offspring of hicks that can't read and can barely listen to English spoken well, and these kids are not used to being roped down for 6 hours a day. There are people here that are glad the kids are in school and that is the parents of those kids. School is free babysitting

The salary for the teacher is small, the town does not have a lot of money but the sheriff and mayor are generous and help off set the lack of money by supplying the teacher with an unlimited account at the sheriff's home brew. Only restriction is that the teacher must be sober during school hours. So far, we had 3 teachers admitted to alcohol rehab from here. Teaching is a very under appreciated profession, but then so is prostitution.

PROPOSALS

Here in Coldbeans, things are different from the real world. Here if we are so lucky as to marry a virgin, that only means that no one outside the family has touched her. She could have three kids and by our standards still be a virgin. One of the greatest attributes in a girl of marrying age is if her mother is sweet and kind. That means that just maybe the girl got some of her mother's genes and is a good catch. One other important attraction is if she had her own teeth, the ones she was born with not the store bought kind! Having big feet is also a good sign and it means that she can pull a bigger plow than the weaker girls can.

The standards for a husband are a bit different. First off he has to be single at the time he proposes. The courtship is less complicated then. It is nice but not required that he have no children of his own. It is also a plus if he is not engaged to anyone else at the time he proposes.
It is hoped by both sets of parents that the wedded couple stay married at least 3 years. Most do but some only last about a week. Parents hate

to go to the effort of cleaning their house for a wedding that only last a month or so. It is sad that the preacher works for free or donations, she could get rich.

Women here love a wedding, Sometimes it is the groom that cries and not the bride. I guess you have your traditions where you live also, but probably not the same ones we have here.

MEMORIES

To many adults, the worse part of the day is getting up to go to work. Not here, here the worst part is when the kids get home from school. In normal homes, usually the only adult home is the mother but here in Coldbeans, since work is on the farm, both parents are home. Now the kids know when they get home, they are supposed to start on the farm chores but when has a kid volunteered to go straight to work? First thing a kid wants to do is work off some of that stored energy by playing. The wiser parents let the kids go out for awhile and romp and play and do all the things that normal kids do, but come chore time, it is time to switch hats and change from boy to farm helper. Learning that life is not all play is a hard thing for kids to do, but it is a necessary lesson to learn. No normal kid will stop play to do chores willingly. It is sad that growing up must interfere with the idyllic life of youth but we all must do it. The nice part is that from time to time, we can visit the theater of the mind and remember all those nice times.

Kids don't know that adults want to think back to the good old days, just like the kids want to. Memories are great and it is good memories that we chose to keep in our mental lock box. We should be happy that we have those memories and from time to time, go back to the halcyon days of yesteryear.

SPRING IS FOR PLAYING

What adult wants to leap out of bed and is eager to get to work. No one I know thinks like that. For a kid, having to leave a warm bed on a cold morning is the worse torture possible. If dad got up and stoked the fire, it is warm and toasty and soft and comfortable under that quilt.

In the summer, things are different; the place is still cool in the morning with the shade of the big tree keeping the sun away from the house. But summer time means exploring it is adventure time, find new trees to climb, check out the creek for crawdads, and chase butterflies. In other words spring is designed for kids. But there is a fly in the ointment. Someone made spring not only a time to play but also planting time. If you don't plant, there is no crop to last through the winter so preparing the fields for planting is part of spring. That is the problem with the world; there is always some kind of work to interfere with the fun of being a kid.

Want to know a secret? The adults will not admit it, but they agree with you. Not all adults have forgotten what it was like being a kid in the spring. So… A little leeway is allowed, just a bit of burning off energy before the evil chores must be done. In truth no parent has let go of the child from his or her own youth. They remember those days and thru their children they can relive the halcyon days of long ago and for a few minutes return to their own youth.

FAMILY PETS

Every family here has a dog for hunting and for the kids to play with. Some of the dogs sleep in the house, often in bed with one of the kids and other days sleep under the house if it is raised off the ground. I think they prefer the under the house thing cause sleeping with a kid means not a lot of rest.

Dogs earn their keep here. They are the perfect companions for a kid and they guard their territory as if they were making the payments. They go hunting and love the challenge of the hunt. On the other hand, cats sleep and maybe will watch a mouse go by. Cats by nature sleep a lot. Unlike dogs, cats care less about what is going on unless it is the sound of a can of food being opened. A dog is a boy's best companion and together they can romp and play all day. I am trying to think of what use a cat is to the home! Dogs wake up ready to play, cats wake up to turn around and go back to sleep.

Don't compare cats with women, a cat is indifferent to the world and a woman runs the world from at home. Never have a pet that does not earn its keep. Dogs hunt and play with the boys. Cats hunt and keep the wife happy. Keeping the wife happy is reward enough to put up with a cat. What kind of pet you like is not important, it is only important that the pet makes you happy.

TIME

Well, it is daylight savings time again. So what do you do with all that daylight you save? I wonder how the animals cope with having to rise later and go to bed at a different time.

Time is an invention of man, animals know when it is day and when it is night and don't worry about the in between. We are on time, spend time and waste time but the animals just go on as if time and humans do not matter.

We do not adhere to our internal clock, we have to be to work on time, leave for lunch on time and be home on time, but not here in Coldbeans. Time in Coldbeans is for the most part governed by the seasons, not the hours. We know when it is daylight, to get up and most of us have enough sense to know if it is a workday or a Sunday. We know when it is dark and is super time and to be on time. That is all the time keeping we need. In other words, we march to a different drummer. We are not slaves to set time as you city work a day bees do.

The important times here is Church time (on Sundays) planting time, harvest time and wintertime, and just for the kids and the young at heart, spring time. We don't have time for those other times and that gives us time to enjoy our time.

COLDBEANS CLUBS

Coldbeans might be a rural town, but we do have some interesting things. We have several social clubs, mostly for the women. One club meets on Tuesdays to do picture puzzles, or as we call them down here "jigsaw puzzles." Most of you probably have never put together one of them. They are now out of fashion and TV is more interesting. The old ones (meaning the better ones) were mostly of paintings of the old masters and you learned an appreciation of the arts while assembling the puzzle. As a kid, I spent many an afternoon with my grandmother, sitting at a card table and putting together a puzzle. She had the good side, she worked from the bottom up, and I sat at the top and worked upside down. Toward the end, we had a running joke that the one who put in the last piece won. It did not take me long to find out that she would hide one piece so that she would win. When both of us did that, there were two pieces missing at the end and one of us had to give in, guess. I lost every time. That is the power of an adult over the child. The puzzles of today are just cheap photos with the color boosted up and thus not the appreciation of the art work that we enjoyed while working on them. Imitation is never as good as the original.

The men's club meets while the women are at their club and it is required that you bring your own beer and enough to share and also your own cigars. The meeting is in the barn because if the wife comes home and the house stinks of cigars, someone will be sleeping either in the barn or under the house with the dogs. We are trying to get the men's club moved to the jail so we can have a bit of the stuff that the sheriff brews. So far he has not been happy with that idea.

Life here is not all plowing and work. We do have our fun and it is safe fun.

PASS IT ON

I enjoy writing about the "old" days of my youth and the things that made me happy and now are gone except for my memory. Think about where you are now and how life has changed for you from the time of your youth until now. You have memories, some that you want to share with your children and if you get the chance, with the grand's as well when they get to an age they can appreciate them. We remember things in small bits, not the whole growing up process at once but the special things that stick out. Record these memories on tape or in writing. When you are gone so are the experiences that made you who you are unless you recorded them.

Pass along to those who follow you that it is their responsibility to pass all this family history on to others in their time. Before writing, history was an oral art and a special person with a talent for remembering fact was assigned the chore of keeping the history. Now with VCR and CD's and all the other methods we can give to our kids a more accurate gift of our life and how we were happy and sad and what make us remember these special things. Family history is special history. It is not taught at school but at home and kids are interested in their parents and how things were done in the "old days."

INVEST IN YOUR KIDS

Kids are born without memory. Memory comes with time and experience. Each child thinks that he was the first one to discover that special fishing place and that special tree to climb. So too with the memory of those special hiding places. All these things are theirs, or so they think. Dad had these same places when he was that age and is it not great that your kid made the same choices that you did?

A kid will follow in his parent's steps until he or she learns to explore his own world. Oh, if we, as adults, could only go back to those days when the world was one great adventure and life was lived to it's fullest. We can relive our youth through our kids and we should pay close attention to their adventures and listen to them when they are excited about "their new discovery"

We give life to our children but they give us life also The life that we had when growing up we lost but now have. been rediscovered thanks to the children. They are our future and also a door to our own past. In them lies the foundation of our family for many generations to come. Prepare them just as you would prepare your garden. A well-kept garden will yield bountiful fruit and so will a well-kept family history.

HAIRCUTS

Working as a barber here in Coldbeans is a tough way to make a living. Most of the men would prefer not to have their hair cut and if they really need it and the wife demands it then he can get the wife to cut if for free and then the wife can't complain about what the cut looks like. The husband can't offer an opinion because after all he didn't want the haircut if the first place so he just keeps his mouth shut and does not look in the mirror.

Of course the at home haircut cuts into Doc's income since his brother is the barber and Shakey can and does sometimes cut more than your hair. In truth, barbering is the only trade in Coldbeans that is in danger of losing it's trade and is the only one that it is dangerous to use. The blacksmith, the general store owner, even the sheriff has no competition for their trade.

Of course the trade we are talking about when we say the sheriff is his home brew. Not only does he make the best but it is also not good to be in competition with the sheriff when you are a shiner! In truth, everyone knows the rules and they are all happy with the status quo. Ain't nothing like a smooth running town.

BOY MEETS GIRLS

Boys live to get out and play; I don't know what girls do. I guess they stay home and help mommies bake a cookie but that is not fun. Fun is climbing trees and looking for places to build a fort or a swing. Young girls and young boys lead separate lives but somewhere around early teenager they discover that maybe, just maybe, girls might be interesting. Boys try to get a girls attention by teasing her mad and making her chase him. Girls get boys interested in them by ignoring the boys. We don't know why but girls are born with this instinct of making the boys interested in them by avoiding the boys, and darn it, it works.

When a girl finally lets the boy catch her, he is ruined for life. He will be her slave and go around all the time trying to do stupid stuff to impress her. He will lose his friends over her. She becomes the reason to hop out of bed and is the last thing he thinks of before going to sleep. We don't know what girls think at that time. A girl is indirect, she will not tell the boy a thing about what she is thinking or how she feels. The boy spends all his time trying to show her how wonderful he is by acting like an idiot. Enjoy those wonderful days of courtship; once she has landed you, you are finished with the good life, and the rest of your time will be spend trying to finally do some thing that she approves of. Don't worry, it will never happen. Eve tempted Adam with the apple but it is the man that suffers from the results of her actions.

THE ASSISTANT

Sometimes, the most stupid of decisions can be quite smart.

One of the smarter dumb kids from this area was just offered a job in Washington working for the junior senator from this state. At first that seems a bit weird with all the available men with bright futures ahead of them why would he pick this 15 watt bulb to be his assistant and handle money? In the first place, a politician never does things that will not benefit him someway. If you think about it when you are in politics, you do not want others to know which hand is in which pocket so you need an assistant that is discreet or stupid or both and unaware of what is happening.

Guess which talent this assistant has? Right, he would not know how to even count much less what to do with the money so he is the perfect assistant After all, the secretary does all the schedules and keeps the notes. His job is to wear a suit, stand there, hand important papers to the senator, and look important. The fact that he does not know what is going on is his great asset and the main reason for being picked for the job. The rule is, never hire anyone smarter than you are. They might take your job, and I can guarantee that the senator's job is safe for the time being.

THE SUBJECT IS WOMEN

In America, it is Majority Rules! Here in Coldbeans, we are not sure that is fair. Here the majority (of those who care) are women. They love to stick their nose in everyone's business. We men are a bit laid back and just let the good times roll. We think that "if it ain't broke don't meddle with it." Women are always busy with meetings and town activities. They like to do things and think of things for US to do. We try to ignore them but that is like trying to get a good night sleep in the cave with a bear. Women just won't leave things alone. They have to solve all the problems of the world. The fact that man is married to a woman is the greatest reason that there has never been a woman president (yet).

We like our women, we don't tell them what to do, when to do it and how to do it, but it ain't the same with women. They think they have a better way to do everything. If they can't do it they will try to make their poor mate do it for them and the way they want it done and not his way of doing it. A woman is the reason that men shave, take a bath, and go to work. But dog gone it, we ain't found a good substitute for women yet! We don't have to agree with them, but we do have to put up with them and at times that can be mighty nice doing.

MORE ON WOMEN

A town meeting is a good example of who runs the place. Seldom do men show up for a town meeting except for the sheriff and the mayor and they have to be there to check up on each other, Just like in a family, the women are the voice of the town. Without women, the town would go to hell in a hand basket. If it were not for women in the home, there would be far less baths, no school and no need for soap. Men would not have to shave and the whole place would be a pigsty. Women are the conscience of this country and the arbitrator of morals and manners. They care for the kids, try to teach them right from wrong and how to be good workers and provide for their own family some day. They try, but it doesn't seem to sink in too well with us men. Women don't teach us to smoke or drink or cuss. We learn that on our own and do a good job of it I must admit. God we love our women but do we have to do what they want us to do? We admit that things turn out better with them in charge, but dang it, the male is SUPPOSED to be the boss. Why do women not get that message!

Until a good substitute comes along, we will just have to do what the women tell us to do and secretly, we kind of enjoy having them do that.

LOOKING FOR DIRECTIONS

Would you like to move to Coldbeans? If you wanted to and could find the land for sale we would welcome you. That is easy for us to say, after all, there is seldom any land for sale here and when there is, kinfolks grab it up or the neighbors buy it to add to their own property. Regardless that you would be the owner, it will carry the name of the original settler of that piece of land.

That is why places like the old "Willford" place is still called the "Old Willford" place even though no Willford has lived there for many generations. Things don't change fast here. In fact only the older people remember why some places have the names they do. Most of the family with that name has moved or forgotten about the property. Forgetting is easy around here. It is remembering that is hard to do. Never ask for directions, you will not understand them, even if you write them down and get a map. Direction are given by the name of the families that lived on the road that you are seeking and reading the mail boxes will not help. . Directions go something like this "You go down the lane, where Red used to live, but he ain't there no more so you pass his place and go about two miles to bill's creek and turn left." "Next, you go to the old Hymen place and ask them for directions to get to Smith's crossroads."

We I guess you get the idea. Best bet is to ask someone to ride along with you and show you the way. Even then, don't expect a direct route as the kid will just want to see some of the places that he don't get to see cause they are so far away. You certainly will enjoy the long ride though it is nice here.

Have a nice visit, you all.

WHAT THE MEN DO

In defense of us men in Coldbeans, we are not lazy. Sure we are laid back a bit and things that we don't think are important do not worry us. We leave the running of the world to our elected crooks in Washington. We leave the handling of money to our real boss, the lady of the house.

We leave the care of the kids to their mother. That leaves the important stuff to us. We let them handle the day-to-day stuff and take the weight off their minds so they can function as they wish. We try to handle the cussing, but the women have taking a liking to it and are starting to use it on us a lot and without cause I mention. We are not the lazy *^&#^ louts that the women say we are.

We do the plowing, and the weeding, we know what to plant, when to plant and how to make it grow. That is a lot of responsibility and if we do our jobs wrong, we don't eat well all year long. As for the kids, well there has not been many successful people from Coldbeans so we don't expect much other than they get married, get out of the house and raise their OWN family. Now who could ask for more?

LOST OUR SHERIFF

We have lost our sheriff. (No, he did not die), but if he is seen he might get shot. Seems he left with one of the prettiest women in the area. She was also married and had two kids and a husband. Sheriff Bart also left a wife and two kids behind. Ain't no way with all of that, we will be seeing him again. The deputy is temporary sheriff but he ain't worth a toot without his uncle running the show. We have to find us a sheriff, an honest one that knows when to ignore something that ain't none of his business. We would also like him to be an experienced moon shiner like sheriff Bart was. Dang it, a pretty woman will always causes trouble. Thank God that most of the women here in Coldbeans are as ugly as a dirt road in a rainstorm.

It ain't easy on Sue's husband either; he is left with two kids to raise and without a mama. That is hard work and also he has to make some money to keep things going. Well, there has never been a rainstorm without a bit of sun afterwards. So Ellie Ann noticed Doug, the jilted husband and I think he will be having help with his family now. Things can go bad and that is not a good thing, but when things go bad there is always a good thing right around the corner. It will take a while for the kids to get to know Ellie but not too long. She is easy to get to know. I don't think Doug will have a problem getting to know her.

CHARLES AND JAKE

We have family feuds here. There are whole families not talking to each other but not the kind of hate that makes people take pot shots at each other. It is just being uncivil to a neighbor.

Only in one case did we have a personal feud between two men. Charles and Jake never got along. To be honest, almost no one liked Jake. They were polite and did not treat him like he was invisible. Charles, and no one called him "Charlie," really and I mean really did not like Jake and he was open about it. Jake tried to be friendly with everyone, but he just never learned how. No matter how hard he tried, no one liked him.

The problem was worse because the two men had to work together at the plant. That did not help the association at all. The more together they were, the further apart in like was each of them. We tried to put oil on troubled waters and help the two of them to get along and in truth Jake was willing to try to be friendly but the problem was he just did not know how.
Jake was like a tennis shoe at a formal wedding. Finally Jake retired and eventually died but the evil between them did not leave when Jake did. In fact this statement proves the depth of hate between the two men to a tea. Charles said that if Jake was laying on the floor, gasping for breath, that he would grab the vacuum and suck his last breath out. Now really folks, that is creative hate carried to the ninth degree.

INBREEDING

Feuding is not a full time occupation here. Sure, there are families that just do not get along but the taking of potshots at each other over the fence is for the movies and a long time ago. It just does not happen much anymore. There are neighbors that do not get along. Most of the time, these neighbors are of the same family, and I mean both sides of each family are close kin. Hey, in the country, you gotta find a mate where you can and sometimes it is close kin.

Inbreeding is supposed to make idiots but around here it is hard to tell if the person is inbred or just plain stupid. The fact that his in-laws and parents are the same people doesn't matter. It is also good to intermarry; it keeps the property in the family and allows the family to expand a bit. Now we don't recommend this for city folks. You guys are not stable enough to take a chance on inbreeding. It could cause an idiot or a politician in the family.

ON THE ROAD

We have two families here that the husbands are traveling salesmen. They are not home often but the money does go in the bank at regular times so there is no complaint from the wife. Once in awhile, the wife would like to see her husband, mostly just to see if he is sending the right amount of money home, or is wasting it on other women. Sometimes, the wife has to get the sheriff to encourage the husband to come home for a visit. The saying that absence makes the heart grow fonder is not appropriate to sales representatives; they do come home but only because they have to. Salesmen are encouraged to come home more often when the wife calls and says, "stay out and make a lot of money, dear". This is the dreaded sign that someone else might be entertaining the wife.

Long distance marriage does not work. Close up marriages most times don't work either but that is another story. If you only come home for the weekend, twice a month, then it is like renting a very expensive motel. One or the other of the couple will be unhappy. Most times, it is not the husband. There are few divorces in Coldbeans, but at times it is better than having to kill the spouse, but consider both options before taking action (Just a wee bit of advice there).

CAR DEALING

It never fails that a dumb Yankee will be out sightseeing in his block long car with more air conditioning than we have in the whole town and he will spot an old car or truck in a shed. His first thought is that the yokel that lives their thinks it is junk and "I can get it real cheap." Now this is a scenario that the "yokel" has been thru before and he will have a bit of fun with this Yankee guy.

The Yankee walks up to the door of the old house and gentle knocks so as not damage the house and waits for the sucker to open the door. He greets the owner of the old vehicle with a very friendly smile and says "you all got yourself an old piece of junk there, if you want, I could take it off your hands and no charge to you." Yankees are generous to a fault ain't they?

"Why sir, that is surely kind of you to offer but I was a hoping to get a bit of money for that old thing" The hook is set and the fun begins. "Well old man, said the Yankee. " Let me look at it and see if I can offer you anything for it, but it looks like it ain't worth much"

"I surely would kindly appreciate you doing that, sir" "I would like to get a bit of money, we ain't got much of that around here you know" "Well old man, I might be able to give you maybe fifty bucks for the thing but it will cost me a lot to try to haul that off, you know" "That's mighty nice of you, being as you are a stranger and willing to help me get rid of that old junk. It ain't been driven since my grandma passed away about 25 years ago" "But you see sir, I was hoping to get a bit more, cause it is old and still runs ok" "Well how much you want for it, old man?"

The old man scratched his head, pondered a bit, and said, "I thought maybe about 3500 bucks, since it is very old and in good condition." The old man was laughing and turned to his wife as the Yankee sped off, "that one got away faster then the other ones" and they both had a good laugh and a sip of "shine" and went back to reading their recent copy of "Antique car" magazine.

STRANGE OUTHOUSE

This may sound stupid but everything in Coldbeans sounds stupid to most people. A friend of mine had to stay over night in the big city and he is not used to all the conveniences they offer. He did the same as if he was home. First he did a bag lunch for supper, (6 beers and a hotdog) and pulled the covers off the bed and slept on the floor. Sometime during the night, the 6 pack called and it was bathroom time. Now Josh was not accustomed to new things like a flushing toilet inside the house and back home the outhouse was a bit far away. He had this habit of just standing in the window and letting it fly outside to the great outdoors.

His bed was right beside the window, so he opened the window climbed up on the sill and all of this action was taking place while drunk and half asleep. He got confused which is not hard for him to do sober but a lot easier when drunk. He got his directions wrong and wet all over his bed and turned around and stepped out the window. He was fortunate; he landed on another drunk and only broke his leg. The other drunk sobered up immediately and ran away. Josh did not quit drinking but he sure did learn to walk to the outhouse when home. He also limps a bit now.

DIFFERENT HABITS

NOTICE (as if you really wanted to know) the Coldbeans café does serve breakfast but not to a lot of people, mostly just the women folks. The men never eat a meal that does not have beer as a beverage. I'm not saying that our men are alcoholics. They just think that coffee is for hangovers only and tea is for Yankees or wimps. We do have different eating habits down here. First we agree that breakfast is a morning meal, best eaten with a hangover. We have dinner as the noon meal, what you call "lunch" Supper is the evening meal. It is as different as peanuts between the "nawth" and the south. We like them boiled and you want the parched. We eat grits with breakfast and sometimes supper. You guys only know about potatoes or rice. Yankees think that possum is a comic strip and that cooter (turtle) is a bug and we call it suppertime. One thing we all agree on, is that we are Americans and damn proud to be one. Don't mess with us.

HELPFUL TIPS AND SIGNS

Planting Garlic around the yard and in the garden will keep out dogs, crooks, salesmen and politicians. Planting garlic around the outhouse will not help, but will save on time spend in there and the reading of the catalog. Putting your name on the neighbor's mailbox will not stop those bills from coning and for sure the neighbor will not pay them. We might be stupid but not that bad (yet). We do not have signs showing how to get to Coldbeans but we have put up one on each road leading out of Coldbeans, saying, GUESS WHAT, YOU JUST MISSED COLDBEANS, and KEEP GOING! There is one sign, just as you enter Coldbeans, saying "all politicians report to the sheriff for immediate arrest!" We don't do a lot of signs but the ones we do are effective.

FARM EDUCATION

If you have been reading this book, you think that kids leap out of bed in the summer and romp and play all day and in the winter, they have to be forced at gunpoint to get up and go to school. That is part right, but that is also universal everywhere. No kid likes to go to school on a cold winter morning or stay in bed on a sunshine day in the summer. Now kids do not like school, not because they are forced to learn but because it interferes with their "discovery" time, the time when they explore and learn. Learning in school is not nearly as much fun as learning outdoors plus sitting all day can be boring. Formal education is necessary to compete in the world but the best laboratory for learning is the great outdoor.

Do not squash the curiosity of a kid. A curios kid is an intelligent kid and kids learn best when they are interested in what they have to learn. A kid would much rather learn the rules of baseball than the history of the United States. Alas, formal education is a necessity in the real world. The day of the dumb clodhopper in the south is over. It takes smarts to run a farm and make enough to feed the family. So, when you look out that car window at the stupid country hick working in his field, remember, he owns the land and he makes a living from it and he is his own boss, (behind his wife, of course)

COME WORK FOR US AWHILE

If you are new at country life, or just visiting, things might be difficult to get used too. If you are from the city and visiting, try a bit of the farm life, most here will put you up for a few days so you can get the experience and they will enjoy the laugh at your expense. First, try a bit of weeding, like 10 or 12 rows about 100 feet long will do fine. Next try a bit of picking okra without itching. Only pick the small pods, the big ones are only good for tent pegs. You can rest by sitting on the porch and shelling peas or beans. Nothing comes ready to cook off the farm.

You think that if you come in the winter, there will not be much to do. How do you think the wood for the stove gets in the house or gets split? Getting up on a cold morning is hard to do, but someone has to be the one to start the fire and surely you don't expect the man to do it! Maybe you think the hogs and the chickens don't eat in the wintertime? Farm work is a labor of love and if you hate it you will never be a farmer. So go to your air-conditioned store and buy the stuff we get to put on our table by our working to make it grow and our eats are fresh.

We don't have a lot of money and we don't waste what we have on stuff we can grow. That is just being poor but not being lazy.

YANKEE TOURIST

It is amusing to see Yankee tourist get off the bus and aim their camera while saying, hey "Harry, look at that dumb yokel over there" "I got to get a picture of this for back home, they would not believe it" We are the ones that should be taking the pictures. These dang tourists have no manners and no tact at all. They are rude and crude. We love it though, we like to act real stupid and drool a bit for the picture. They run around buying all the souvenirs the can find. They love the plates of antebellum homes with a southern belle in front of the main house. What they don't see is the back of the plate where is imprinted in very small letters, "made in China"

The Yankee pointing out the town token redneck with the beer belly, hair uncombed and clodhopper shoes on is dressed much worse than the fellow he is taking a picture of. The Yankee has on a flowered shirt (no beach or water around here) shorts, sandals and a cigarette hanging out his mouth. He has two cameras and a camera bag that would hold week's clothes, but **we** are the ones looking silly? Come on folks, the plantation homes are further south, like in Charleston not here. We were always dirt-poor farmers and never had a big house or slaves and did not want any. Learn about the people you are visiting before going there.

CITY AND COUNTRY

Oyster shell roads are further south, a bit closer to Charleston. Here it is one paved road and mostly dirt roads. The dirt roads, though hard to travel, are the most interesting. There is where the real residents live. Off of the highways and byways of civilization. There are no semi-trucks zooming by and no billboard signs, no freeways, and you think we are stupid. Where do you live, what do you see outside YOUR window?

If you live in a small community, you have to commute to work and face the daily drive on the freeway. Is it worth it to work in the city and drive a long distance to get away from where you work so you can spend a little time outside of the city but surrounded by hundreds of homes just like yours? We walk to work on our own land, and we come home when the work is done and not when the clock strikes 5pm. We are not picking on you for your lifestyle, but we want you to know that we are happy in our place and don't really think you are there. It is all in which end of the binoculars you are looking thru. You would not be happy here and we would not be happy there, so that is why God created more than one flavor of ice cream.

REPLACEMENTS

The new sheriff just isn't working out too well. We knew that he could not do moonshine like the old sheriff but his is awful. Hardly anyone wants to go to jail now. The only good thing he did in this town is make more business for the Red Dot store. People gotta drink and they want good stuff, but if they can't get the really good stuff, then they will buy the legal stuff. The town changes and we have to accept the change.

Change is hard to accept, even for a town locked in a time warp. We look in the mirror daily and notice very little change but one day we look and wonder "where did those wrinkles come from!" Age is a slow worker, and the things we could do just a short while ago are now difficult. The farm does not notice this. The animals still want their food on time and the crops will still ripen even if we are unable to pick them. That is the purpose of raising kids. The next generation will do the things we can't do anymore and they will carry on the work and traditions. We even grow our own replacements here.

HERE COMES THE GUVMINT

It had to happen the town that does not exist will have to "incorporate" according to the state of SC. They don't care if we are real or not, they just want money, taxes and authority and a hand in running everything. I wonder if there is a way to charge the Guvmint for our services, the things that we do for them like look the other way when they are stealing.

A small town with only a mayor, one sheriff, and a dimwit deputy should be enough officials. Now we have to be part of the big bureaucracy and collect taxes so that the state has more money to spend on fewer services to us. Once gain, we are trying to apply logic to guvmint service. We will now have to have more rules, things like "you can't steal unless you are an official" and "you must pay taxes unless taxes pay your salary" Guvmint is as necessary as flea and roaches at home. You got them but you don't want them and you spend money trying to get rid of them and yet they multiply. Look at the laws, there are more laws about what you CAN'T do, then there is about what you can do. Freedom of religion we still have, but freedom from unfair taxes is forever with us.

STINKY JOHNSON

J. C Johnson was the only man in Coldbeans to always have a cold and there was a good reason for that. First, he was one of few men, besides Caleb, that did not like to take a bath. The problem was not his body smell. That was bad but acceptable. The problem was that he never washed his feet. Having a cold helped him to not smell himself and that is why he never tried to cure the cold. Not washing his feet caused another problem for him, besides being very lonely. You see, he knew his feet stunk but taking a bath was worse so being one of the smarter Johnson's he thought to solve the problem by just sleeping with his feet out of the window. This makes it very hard to sleep if you have to turn over during the night and also caused a might bit of a problem for the dog who preferred to sleep under that particular side of the house.

I know that this sounds stupid, but don't forget, J C was the smartest dumb person in Coldbeans, or so he thought. Need I point out that J C lived alone; he never had the pleasure of a woman in his whole life. That meant that he did not have kids to do the farm chores for him. When J C went on his rounds to feed the animals, the hogs got excited when he approached. The cows went to the other side of the pasture and the chickens ran under the house. J C was a very lonely man.

The biggest problem that J C had was in getting supplies. He could not go to town, because no store would let him in and even the horse refused to pull the wagon. It is hard for horses to hold their noses. Supplies were delivered and J C agreed to be elsewhere when they arrived. Even the money that he paid with had to be washed before it could be used again.

When J C finally died special provisions was made for the pallbearers. They were allowed to hold the coffin with one hand and their nose with the other. It was considered to just cremate J C but they were afraid that they could not get the fire out afterwards. After the burial and for a year or so, nothing would grow or survive for 20 feet around his grave.

CLARA

Is there only one Caleb? Sadly, there is also a female version of Caleb. They are no kin and rarely see each other and woe to the person near by when they do meet. In all honesty, Clara is not as bad as Caleb, but who can measure stink? She does bathe, one thing that Caleb hates to do but Clara, being a large woman can't reach her feet so they are the part of her that smells. Since she is (to be generous) as ugly as the south end of a north bound mule, she has only a few friends and none that would want to be there when she does bathe. Bathing is not one of the favorite things to do here in Coldbeans because of the trouble you have to go to with heating the water and all that but most people (women) know that it has to be done. We must bath at least once a week for church anyway, but seldom do people bathe every day. If cleanliness is next to Godliness, then there are a few heathens here. Going by those standards hell must really stink.

WHO ARE THE DUMB ONES?

I have been thinking, Coldbeans being a mythical town. Even though it does not exist, it could. It has many strange people living here. I wonder how so many weirdoes' came to be at the same spot and formed a community like we did?

At first glance I thought this town was the weirdest spot on earth and the craziest people alive. That is until I visited Washington. Strange as it may seem, the residents that live there and run our country, are weirder than any living in our tiny town and what is worse is that we pay those people to live there and to take care of our money and our nation. With this thought comes the disturbing conclusion that the people of Washington are a lot smarter than us. We pay them to be stupid and here we do it for free. I think the residents of Coldbeans could do just as good a job of running the country and do it a lot cheaper. The problem might come about when people from other countries come to visit and see who is in charge. Wait a minute, they laugh at us NOW!

INNOCENT CHILDREN

Some children would be better off without parents. I don't mean that they have to be orphaned but that the influence of adults can sometimes have a bad effect on kids. Kids, with few exceptions, are born innocent. The circumstances of their birth are not important to them. They just want a chance to live and grow up. The influence of adults on kids can be good or bad. They can instill values and a sense of morality or raise their children to be a slave for the parents. A child must be taught to think badly. He or she is not born with that view. Adults should listen to the children. They see things in ways that we have lost as we matured. A child view is untainted by the adult mind. They are truly seeing things we cannot see. Children see the world as bright and a place to explore and learn, not as a harmful place that is dangerous to them. That part is our job to teach. We must protect the children as they grow but we must be careful to not harm them or enslave them.

Let these fresh minds become the new way of thinking in the world. Molding them in our fashion will only carry on the wrongs that WE

149

do. This is true in Coldbeans, or any other place in the whole world. Children, for the most part, are not born bad, it is us that make them bad or good. God bless America and the people that live here

A CHANGING WORLD

The world is changing, and we, the adults think it is for the better. That is wrong. The world if run by the kids of today would be much better than the corrupt world we give them. Times are changing faster than we adults can adjust. New ways of doing things, ways that we don't understand, are becoming normal to the kids of today. Within less than 20 years, handwriting will be "the old way" of recording information.

There are already devices that can record and print as we talk. But even print is old fashioned. Electronic memory will hold more and do faster and not require the destruction of trees to make paper to make notes that we won't need because it will all be recorded electronic. Kits take a calculator to school. They can do math in ways that we adults had to spend lots of paper making mistakes just to get to the right answer. Any fact that ever happened can be found recorded somewhere, all we need is a retrieval device.

The world is changing, not for the better, but for quicker and easier ways of having information. Learning information is the schools responsibility, well now it will be available not from the teacher but from instant retrieval by the student for his own purpose. When we ask questions, it is because we want to know and having something and having access to the answer to those questions is now available to anyone. It is a new world, one I can't even imagine in my old way of thinking. To the children of today, it is just a logical way of learning. Having information does not mean that we have to use it, but having it available at anytime means that it is there when wanted. It is a brave new world, and we are the past.

AUTOMOBILES

Most of the time, if you see a new car, it is a tourist sightseeing. No one here ever buys a new car, We just can't afford it. We buy someone's car or truck when they can't drive any more. We are honest here and would never sell a piece of junk to someone that we know and will be seeing often. New and used car dealers would starve here. Most of us trust the old four-foot transportation (the mule or the horse).

If you get drunk (and people do here in Coldbeans) and elsewhere too, they can't drive but the can ride even if it is a buggy and the horse knows where he is going. Horses are smart they don't get drunk and do remember how to get back to the stall and the feedbag. The trouble comes not from getting home but what is waiting there for you?. It is universal that the drunker you are the meaner and uglier then waiting wife is.

New cars cost in the use of gas and we don't have much here and it is old stuff and no good even for lighting a fire. Besides, if you want to ride in a car you want to ride better on a paved road and not the dirt ruts we have for roads. Having bad roads keeps down the traveling salesmen visits. If you have a new car and are near by, drive on over and let us see what one looks like, you hear?

THE LOSS OF CHILDHOOD

No matter where you live there are a lot of things universal to raising a family. Tell the truth! How many times have you told your kids NOT to run in the house? Now think before you answer the next question, how many times has that been said to you and how many times did you obey? There is a time that the child crosses a line that he or she can never return. Once you are a parent, you have to see things different and that is sad. No one sees the world like thru a child's eyes. Oh, if we could go back to those days when the world was innocent and we could explore and learn new things everyday. When we lose the view seen through a child's eyes, we lose something precious.

A child hops out of bed in the morning ready to explore. Well, to tell the total truth that does not happen on a school day but let summer come and they are up at sunrise. If we, as adults could only maintain that fresh zeal, that desire to learn, but alas, we now have to work and earn the living so that our kids can do the things that we wish we could still do. If the world were made up of kids only, we would not have all the troubles we now have, war, oppression, greed, murder and all the other things that adults who can't fit in to society have. Sadly, there is no Peter Pan. We must all grown up and have our own kids, and through them we can relive our own childhood. That is what being a parent is about. Be it the big city or here in Coldbeans, parents and kids are the same.

COCA COLA AND THE FESTIVAL

Coldbeans has its annual spring festival and everyone contributes something. The wife and I decided to take the pony; her name was Coca cola, to the festival and give pony rides. I hitched the trailer to the truck and loaded coke into the back and my wife drove the truck and my daughter and I to the festival. The wife was supposed to come back and bring us home afterwards. Of course, daddy did most of the work (my daughter walked the pony a few times but the excitement of that wore off quick and she went looking at the other things). The event was down at the church and on the side we had a place to walk the pony up and down once for each child. By the end of the festival my legs were tight as iron bands and I was tired but had lots of fun with the little kids who had never been on a pony. It was different from the mules that they rode back home. We waited for the truck and trailer to show up and take us home. Coke did not seem to mind, and she had done most of the work walking up and down, up and down. Good thing she was not smart and she enjoyed the kids on her back. The wife finally showed up with the truck and the trailer. She seemed stressed and said we would get an explanation when we got home.

The story was that our white cat (which was born deaf) had crawled up into the engine of the truck and went to sleep. Starting a truck engine while a cat is asleep on the motor is not good for the cat and worse when the cat got its ear caught in the fan belt and about tore the ear off. It also makes a lot of noise. It did the motor of the truck no good either; the fan belt was twisted and was so tight that the engine would not start. Thanks for the neighbor being home or we would probably still be still waiting for the transportation to show up.

Well we got home, and coke was put into her pasture, much to her delight. We went searching for the cat. We could not find her anywhere. Later on that day, I got an idea of a place I had not looked because I never thought a cat would be so stupid as to do the same thing twice, but sure enough, I found her inside the other car, scared to death. The cost of the trip to the vet was way more than that cat was worth. We can look back on disaster with good memories after the event is over. I don't know if a cat has long memory but I don't think she will ever sleep on a motor again.

COCA COLA REVISITED

Coke was a mare and the man we got her from someone who only used her to tease the real horses for breeding to full size mares. We decided to make coke a mother so we borrowed a male pony and had her bred. My wife was beside herself with hopes that she could be there when the baby came. She got home from work one day and as usual, went out to the pasture to check on coke. She was a bit too late. Coke was already a mother and was doing her job well: the baby was nursing just find. Nature s animals rarely need any training. Life and creation is a natural thing to them.

One day the neighbor came over with her visiting grandson and wanted to show the kid the new baby pony. Coke and the baby were down in the back pasture and we walked down and sure enough, it was dinnertime for the baby. The kid, who had never been on a farm and had never seen an animal up close,. He was all wide-eyed and very interested in what was happening. He turned to his grandmother and asked innocently "what's he doing?" The grandmother explained that the baby was drinking his milk.

Now this city kid was not stupid, he could not be fooled. He looked at his grandmother like she was crazy and said "you don't get milk from a horse; you get milk from a cow! Try explaining that to a 5 year old!

CHARLIE'S ADVENTURE

Charlie was my favorite dog of all times. He was a German Sheppard just like hundred of other farm dogs and he and the kids go along great.

He would follow the kids everywhere and never seemed to get tired. When I went to town, he would hop into the bed of the truck, or if the wife was not going, he rode in the front seat. One day, Charlie and I went to town and when I came back out from the store, Charlie was gone. I looked for him and call his name but had no luck so I had to get home with the stuff and get it in the refrigerator before it melted. Next morning, there still was no Charlie and I got worried. He had never stayed out like this and he knew his way home on his own.

Two weeks went by and Charlie was home. Of course he could not explain where he had been, he was not that smart but we were glad to see him and that he was ok. Charlie and I continued our trips to town and Charlie would leave and be back at the truck on time. About two months later, Charlie and I took a trip to town and Charlie took off as usual, I figured that he had things to do and places to see and that as usual, he would be back on time. When I came out of the store and loaded the truck Charlie showed up and unlike any time before, this time he looked straight at me and barked. He then turned and walked off a piece and turned and barked again.

I may just be a stupid human but even I could see that Charlie had something to show me. Around the corner and besides the building I met his interest. A beautiful collie and she was not the only reason for Charlie's interest. There was the cutest litter of puppies you ever saw. They were intelligent like their dad and pretty like their mother. The collies' owner agreed to share the pups after they were weaned.

Charlie now has offspring of his own to teach the art of running a farm and controlling the animals that are in "his" charge. Proud parents are everywhere, even in the animal world.

YOU TO CAN SAVE THE PAST

To those that say they wish they could write, hey. You can! Writing is easy, it is just thinking with your fingers if you type or if you don't type, then talk to a recorder or write longhand. The most important thing is to record your thoughts. Re live past times or tell lies and make up things that you WISHED you could have done. The important thing is to put down on paper things that are important to you and might be important to someone else later on. You may not know who that someone might be but he or she will be sharing in your memories and maybe enjoying the same feeling that you had. Don't you wish that you had spent some time with your grandmother or grandfather and heard of all the adventures that they had when they were young? History is not all about learning who was president at some time long ago and who shot whom. It is also your HERITAGE.

The family history stops with the person who did not pay attention when their family was recounting their adventures. Please, keep records of events and keep photos and record on the back what they were. We look at old photos of our parents and our grandparents and wonder why did they take that picture? Why do you take pictures? You do it so you can remember an event, and there is a reason for recording it so make sure that others know so they can also share.

SUMMER HEAT

If you are planning a visit to the south please don't come to Coldbeans, it is a small rural town and not typical of the real south, or the south as envisioned by people who have never been here. Go to a quaint and quiet town with nicely painted homes that have porches that wrap around three sides, or even the large southern homes that are two or three stories and have "verandas." Old homes had high ceilings which helped keep the heat up near the top and made it a bit better to survive in the southern summer heat.

Fans were placed in windows upstairs and since heat likes to rise, it would go up and exit the window and create a bit of breeze downstairs. There was also a cleaver way to cool the homes of rich people from the summer heat. They used heat to cool the house. Mad you say? Well no, it was a vent in the top of the house with gas heat and when it got hot up there, it pulled the heat from downstairs and also pulled in cooler air into the lower windows. Who said southerners were not smart? Of course none of this helped with the humidity. That was the purpose of always having a glass of iced tea in your hand.

Ice was delivered every day by horse and wagon. The homes had high ceilings, 10 or 12 feet high and that keep a bit of the heat up and away from people but all in all no matter what you did it got hot in the south in the summer. If you were born here, you got used to it.

CHOOSING THE RIGHT WIFE

If you are living in the big city, you have to think different from us here in the small towns. First thing is that in small town America marrying is meant forever. Divorces do happen but are frowned on and the town feels like the couple didn't try hard enough. In the big city, a beautiful wife is a treasure. Here it is a liability, there are those who like what others have and they may not stand a snowballs chance in Washington to get her but they can dream and marriages do fall apart because what you got you can't keep.

Here the ideal woman is a plain woman, no pretenses and with all her teeth and a good strong body. Like I just said, standards are different. We go for the long haul and want a woman who will be there to raise the brats and wash and cook and hopefully not nag too much. We feel that a piglet is cute as a button but a hog is ugly to the bone. A wife here has to be more than a status symbol. She has to cook, wash, take care of the kids and make clothes, keep house and control the little money they have. Also once in awhile she needs a strong body to go drag her husband home from getting out with the boys. It ain't no piece of cake to be a farm wife. It is best to pick someone from around where you live but even that might not be good. It is according to how far your own reputation extends.

YOU ARE A STRANGER

A city slicker stands out here like a pig in a dog pound. They just are "different." I guess the same is true if we were to go to Washington. People would think we were not from there or had been elected to serve there. Either way, it would not be a friendly place. Now we like you city folks coming here and taking your pictures. We like the money that you spend on "souvenirs" and most of all, we like it when you leave. In truth, that is the best part to us. "Come on down and visit but don't stay too long". The peculiar thing is we don't see what you see so interesting here. We are just normal people, living normal lives. By the way no one here is named "hayseed" or "hey Rube". We address you as sir and are polite because that is what our parents taught us. I guess yours taught you a bit different.

The United States is a large country and the south is only one part of it but folks seem to think this part of the country never progressed or got away from slavery. We know lots of the same things you know but they are not as important to us as the day-to-day goings on with our neighbors and family. We might seem short sighted, but our view starts here and extends out to everywhere. To us we are the center of our world. One thing you and I can agree on, is "God Bless America, and don't mess with her around me. We thank you, very much.

REMEMBER RADIO?

My generation remembers the wonderful days of Radio. You could do things on radio that is hard to duplicate on TV. The theater of the mind can take you places that Television cannot. Each listener could see his or her hero or the story setting in his or her own mind. The hero was who you wanted them to be, short, tall, dark hair or even bald. You were the director and the radio was the producer.

In the theater of the mind, you could be in outer space or back in history, any place in location or time that you wished. We had fibber Magee and Molly, the Lone Ranger, Hop along Cassidy, Red Skeleton, bob Hope and so many more that could come into your world and you could just listen, you did not have to be there, you could be in the next room ironing or washing clothes and you were still entertained. We still have radio, but only for the news and the noise we sometimes call music. We have lost our innocence and our imagination.

In the name of progress, we have stepped backwards. Entertainment always has to do new things to keep our interest. Exposure to the naked body is not really entertainment. It is voyeurism. Talent is the key to getting our attention, not flares, loud music and explosions. Thru radio, even adults could be kids in their own minds. TV makes us all animals.

Lets try to make life more enjoyable, let the world know that we are not happy with the direction we are taking the taste of our entertainment,

AWAKE WITH FAITH

In every community, town or city, you can find the same people, some successful, others are deadbeats, and the poor are just trying to survive. Here in Coldbeans, we don't really have any of what you might call successful people unless you mean that the land has been worked and the family fed and the bank did not take anything away. By our standard, that is success. I guess.

it is everyone's desire to accumulate money and someday be rich or at least independent. Being a realist and living here long enough, we don't dream that anymore. We just try to survive, raise our kids and hope they continue to hold on to the family land and maybe one day, one of them will be rich. It is only a dream and we would be the first ones surprised if that did happen.

You must believe in the future, you must believe when you first look at your newborn that one day he or she will change the world. You must believe that during you lifetime, you will do something that will help someone later on in life. Dreams and ambitions are what make us get out of bed in the morning and try to make it through another day and have hope for a better tomorrow. We do the best we can, be it a poor farmer, a big business tycoon, the mayor, or the blacksmith. A belief in the future is the reason for getting up and having hope. This is universal, not just for us country folks. God bless our country and help us to a better tomorrow.

COSMO'S MONEY

Cosmo was the perfect image of the southern gentleman. With his mustache and goatee and the soft southern voice he could charm any lady into blushing. Cosmo was too good to live in Coldbeans. He lived just outside of the city limits and in a fine house, two stories with indoor bathrooms on each floor. He even had a car and a garage to put it in. In this way he was not the image of a resident of Coldbeans; He was too rich for Coldbeans. Cosmo lived so high on the hog that the hog did not know he was being eaten.

Cosmo was a charmer and no woman could resist the soft southern drawl and the twinkle in his eye. Unfortunately, for the women of Coldbeans he cottoned to a higher class of women. Those that took a bath every day, wore makeup, and blushed a lot. In other words, no one in Coldbeans qualified. There were a lot of women that tried to qualify. But you can't put a possum in a raccoon suit and believe that it is a raccoon.

We don't know why Cosmo came to live where he did. He had the money to live anywhere he wanted to. No one ever asked Cosmo why and frankly most did not care. He was here so that was that in our way of thinking. Thinking is hard work and if you don't have to it is best not to. Cosmo died (every one does even the rich) and he left a pile of money to the town of Coldbeans but only to be spent in a way approved by his estate. NO money to be spent on Alcohol, no money to be spent on improvements to the town itself. All of the money would go to the school in hopes that someday someone intelligent would emerge from this town and make us and the late Cosmo proud.

It has been five years since we got the money and the people that run the town has yet to figure out how to spend it proper and still be within the stipulations of the will. It is not just the spending, we can do that. It is finding a kid who will make the late Cosmo and us proud.

JERRY JOINED THE ARMY

Jerry joined the Army. It was something that he had wanted to do since he saw Sgt Bilko on the new TV. It looked like fun. They did the same things he did, walk, but they called it "marching", they shot rifles and did not have to pay for the ammo and they got their clothes for free and best of all they wore boots. So Jerry enlisted and was sent to Fort Jackson up in the middle of the state. Jerry thought he had died and gone to heaven. They fed him, gave him new clothes and a place to stay and did not charge a plug nickel for the whole thing. What could be a better deal?

He found out the next morning. Some idiot came around and woke everyone up and it was still dark. Jerry did not mind getting up early but this was not way to wake people up. Then to his surprise, he found out he was the one who had to make his own bed, something he had never done. It was all worth the effort because when he got dressed and they took him to eat, he was in hog heaven. He had never seen such food and so much of it too. Only dang thing wrong was that a guy did not have time to eat properly and was kicked out after only one serving.

When he got back to the barracks, his bed was a mess and Jerry wanted to find out who did it and he was going to kick that fellow from here to sunrise His new Sergeant volunteered that HE had done it and to re-make it and the covers had to be tight or else. Jerry was now getting a bit sick of this hotel and the way they treated the people who stayed in it. He forgot about all of this when they were marched out to get their new rifles. Now this was why he joined in the first place. It was a chance for him to shoot and not have to buy the ammo. When he finally got to go to the rifle range he did not like that they made them walk so far and in step too. Heck his step was longer than the guy in front and he kept bumping into him.

Once on the range dang it there were more rules. You did not just get some bullets and go shoot. The targets were large and not far away. He could almost throw that far. Jerry was a good shot and could hit the "bull's-eye' every time. Only thing was that dang Sergeant wanted him to shoot like everyone else, lying down and in what they called the "prone position" Heck, anyone could shoot like that, but it would be hard to kill a deer lying down. Rapidly, Jerry and the Army came to the same view that they did not agree with each other. Jerry hated to turn in his nice clothes and give back his boots but he was a bit disappointed in this man's Army. They parted friends, and he never saw the expression of relief on the faces of the sergeants he left behind when he got on the bus back to Coldbeans. Ah, home, there is no place like home.

BATHING

Taking a bath if you have a shower is nice and taking a bath in a tub is also nice also but only if the water is piped into your house and you have a hot water heater. It is a bit harder to take a bath in the country. It is also harder to WANT TO take a bath in the country. With all the trouble you have to go to, bringing the water into the house and heating the water and gathering of the wood to heat that water, it is sometimes easier to just go dirty. Easier on you that is, the other folks may not agree. Even after the bath is over and you are dry, there is the problem of getting that dirty water out of the house. Water is heavy you know.

You can ask the kids to do it, but that is only if you want water sloshed all over the kitchen floor on the way out the door. A kid always finds the easiest way to do a chore and easy is not always the best way. At least the water can be put to good use on the flowers or lawn etc. We never do something just to have something to do. There is a reason for everything we do or we don't do it. So we make the most of each action. Never wash only one person, use the water till it is dirty. Reuse the water on the flowers or lawn. Make the most of what you do.

A small country farm is a marvel of efficiency. It is getting the most work for the least effort and at the least cost. We don't have a lot of money but if we have kids, we have free help, not willing help but free. Warning, never tell a kid that when he gets home from school there are some chores you want him to do. He will stay after school and loiter with his friends or go for a walk in the woods; home is the very last place he will go.
Working hard is a way of life in the country but thinking hard makes the work a bit easier to do.

WALKING

Walking is good for you but only if you don't have to walk. If you have to go from one place to another, that is not a pleasant time if you are only walking to get there. But if you are walking without purpose, you can stop as you wish and enjoy a new site or a new view. You can stop and smell the wildflowers or observe quietly the wildlife that you do not see when hurrying from point to point. The same goes for riding in a car. If you have to get somewhere all that in between where you started and where you are going is a blur and wasted time. Make that same trip without having a timetable for getting there and the view is completely different.

The same goes with life. If you hurry to grow up, you miss a lot of the growing up part. That is missing the best years of your life. As the saying goes take time to stop and smell the roses and all the other delights of childhood too. The path from childhood is a one-way street and cannot be taken in reverse. Enjoy that time while you can. You only have one chance at life, make it a good one

GETTING SICK

Getting sick in Coldbeans means a trip to our only doctor and a hope that he is sober when we get there. We once had a good root doctor here and everyone went to her but she died from root poisoning. Strange thing is that the spot where we buried her, a tree grew and no one knows what kind of tree it is.

To get to the town doctor means a trip in the family car if you have one or the horse and wagon. Neither one is good if you feel bad. Most just want to stay under the cover and take some homemade medicine and sleep. That works for some things but not for the real ills. Doc is your best bet if he is sober. If he knows you are paying in cash, he will rush you ahead of the other people in the waiting room.

Since Coldbeans has no drugstore, Doc prescribes the meds and also sells them to you. This cuts down on his patient charge. No one has died from visiting Doc but a few have wanted to get better so they could go kill him. Once better, they changed their minds though. The nice thing is that country folks don't get sick often or won't admit it.

INDIANS

Let me see, doctor, lawyer, Indian chief. Most of them we have. We no longer have a lawyer because we promoted him to judge to keep him from cheating so many people There is no Indian chief here, in fact there are no Indians here but there is one guy who pretends to be an Indian for the tourist but he is not a real Indian. South Carolina had lots of Indian tribes but most blended in with the new "locals" over the years. In truth, almost all of Coldbeans are immigrants somewhere in their past.

This area was a wilderness until settled by Moses Clapwater back in 1726. We are all descendants of old "clappy" or have migrated from other small town around. We can honestly say that to our knowledge, we have no Yankee blood in any of us. Yankees make good tourist, they spend money and laugh at us but when they are gone we laugh at them too. The area is filling up and the people of Coldbeans are mingling with the people from other towns and so the families are becoming more widespread and we are getting new blood.

We have a diverse group of Indians in South Carolina. We have Cherokees, Ogeechees, Yamacaw and many others. Unlike the old days Indians are now respected and proud of their background and people brag now about having a little Indian blood in them. There was a time they were called half-breeds but now every one is proud of his or her heritage. After all, the Indians were here first, we are the new people.

SWEET SMELLING BOYS

You would think that improvements to life styles would be a good thing. We followed the trend here and had the well connected to the house so that we would not have to carry water in and heat it. We even got a gas hot water heater too. We felt like rich city folks.

Well for every "convenience" there is a minus side. Having water come into the new bathroom made it more fun to take a bath. That was fine for the girls, they love to smell pretty for the boys but when the boys started bathing every morning before going to school, we decided to have a sit-down talk with them. It seems that boys who don't smell are more attractive to the girls and they become popular. The other boys (the "normal" ones) were out of luck for attention because according to the girls, "those guys stunk"

Having competition for the girls makes the more forward boys a bit nervous and they went around warning the "smell good" kids to not bathe or get beat up. School is a high-pressure social environment even at normal, but when the girls all want boys that "smell good". Well then, trouble is a brewing. One of the smarter boys, and I won't admit that he was mine, but he came up with a good idea. He told the "stinkers" that if they took a bath the girls would like them also and as a bonus they would not have trouble with fleas itching or flies. Slowly, one by one, the boys cottoned to the idea and soon the school smelled like a flower shop, which turned the girls off because now the boys smelled better than the girls did. When it comes to "women" you can't win.

TOP OF THE CLASS

Jon graduated first in his class and was vote most likely to succeed. Jon graduated 31 years ago and to this date he has done nothing right. Jon was only 18 when he graduated high school. His was a promising life but as with a lot of people some of them don't live up to the promise. Jon's problem was that when he graduated, he had become a father 3 times over and that meant going to work wherever he could find it. His first girl friend had a baby by him when he was only 16 and the second girl friend had a "boo- boo" twice by him thus the title of father meant that as soon as he was out of school, it was earn that paycheck and give it to the mothers of his children. Alas, many a career has been cut short by early fatherhood. Sometimes the "'FATHER" is not the real "father" but a better provider than the real one was.

The mother to be is obvious but the father is often whoever the girl "thinks" it is or someone that she would LIKE to see be the father. Anyway, Jon never made it in the business world but he did learn a big lesson. He never again became a father. He still bags groceries at the local general store and is poor but happy now.

THE GOOD SIDE OF DRINKING

If you have been lucky to tour our town and been invited into a few homes you might think we are rich with all the "antiques' lying around.

These are not antiques to us, they are just the "hand me downs" from our parents and their parents and are used every day. The cast iron pot and the cast iron skillet are highly collectable in the big city world, but here they are working pieces and used daily.

Nothing cooks like cast iron. It heats up rapidly and holds its heat. It does not dent or warp. It is heavy and a bit hard on the frail women but there are no frail women here. Most of our women can arm wrestle a man and toss him 29 feet out of the house if she is made mad enough. A mad woman is slow to cool down. It is best to go to the woodpile and chop some wood or to the barn and hide or even better to go to town and have a drink or two or three. Coming home drunk won't matter, you are gonna get whipped anyway so you might as well not feel it or remember it when you wake up. Patience and a bit of the devils brew helps keep the marriage together. Have you noticed that ONLY the men have to drink? The women are just as happy sober as we are drunk. That should say something about marriage.

A MAN'S PUNISHMENT

It is generally agreed also that women for the most part are mean and controlling. Men on the other hand, are considered lazy and drunks. There must be a reason for the difference other than the sex. Men are more laid back and accept things. Women on the other hand make the rules and the rules do not change. The amazing things are most women make the same rules and most men do not want to obey those same rules.

There are hard and fast thoughts on what the two sexes have to do. The men labor and make the money, the women spend it. That much we can all agree on. Now in the big city the women work hard and make money also and some have to take care of lazy men that will not work. This is the fault of those women. A man that won't work would not eat in a home here. He would find himself competing for a bed with the dogs under the house. I guess if you are raised in a hard life, then you don't cotton to lazy or weak husbands.

In defense of the men, and I am one. We have to be on our toes all the time to make sure that we don't get bashed up side the head and have no idea why. That is, assuming that we can think after being bashed. Now you city folks might find this horrible because you have something called "spousal abuse" Here it is looked on a bit different, "shape up, do your part or get out",

Spending time in jail is not punishment, they feed you, clothe you and your wife can't get to you to beat you up again. So what is the punishment?

GOOD RULES TO FOLLOW

There are rules everywhere you go. The rules are different in the city as opposed to the country. Her are a few.

1. Never shoot someone in a home where you are a guest.
2. Chewing bacca is frowned in church, wait till you are outside.
3. Always wear clean underwear when company is expected.
4. The driver has first choice at a dead possum in the road.
5. When at church, compliment the women, even if they are ugly and you have to lie.
6. If you win at poker, don't bring the money home. That would be a waste of good luck.

Now for the best rule of all. Always put the horse or mule at the front of the wagon. Put the jackass at the back and tell her to keep quiet.

ADVICE TO THE READERS

I have been talking about all the weird people that live in Coldbeans, but not a bit about me. First, I should not have been born here; my tastes are much too good for this area.

I enjoy taking a bath every week and even use soap. Unlike most of the men, I wear socks with my shoes and I almost never go barefooted except in the shower. To me, Labor is a political party in Great Britain and not real work. Hard labor is for uneducated people. Smart people don't have to work; they can get rich off of the poor people or get welfare. I don't have a lot of money nor do I have enough women but I survive on what I can get, trick or fool. Being able to read and write gives one a great advantage in Coldbeans, it makes you tower over the illiterate, of which there are so many.

As the saying goes, "a one eyed man is the king in a place of blind people" thus in Coldbeans, I am the only one capable of writing about this place, what the heck, the truth is that I am the only one capable of writing in this whole place. Now that you know me, go back and read some of the stories that are in this book and understand them better. Study hard; get a job, pay your taxes or you to could end up living in a Coldbeans of your own.

PARADOX OF OUR TIME

It is a great paradox that men can invent armor to protect soldiers so they can kill the enemy safer but no one can invent a car that is safe to drive on the freeway. We have taller building, longer lines and more hungry people in the world of tomorrow as seen from 20 years ago. More minds are busy trying to find better ways of killing people and not better ways of keeping us alive. We have bigger and wider road so that we can drive our cars that run on foreign oil more slowly and have more congestion and accidents. We now turn out smarter people from college so that they can't find a job because they want to live in America and not in India. We buy more from overseas and sell less to other countries. We have unions so that we can work and then can't work because the union is on strike.

Do you find something wrong with this logic, or can you really call it logic? And you think we country bumpkins are stupid

SPOUSAL ABUSE

Spousal abuse is not unique to the big city and all their stress. We have it here in Coldbeans, just like everywhere else. It is hard for two people to live together without once in a while for tempers to flare, but physical harm is another thing. Most men here have learned over the years how to avoid spousal abuse. They just keep their mouth shut and go have a drink. Sometimes the abuser follows and there is no avoiding it. Most times he is not hurt a lot and a quick drink of likker will ease the pain, but not the suffering, that will go on until she calms down. In the worse cases, doc is called out and he brings the sheriff, for his own protect, not for the injured party.

The couple has a bit of time to reflect on what went wrong, that is when did he opens his mouth and say something that caused her to get madder than she was already. This happens only when the marriage is fairly new, that is the first 10 years. After that, he has learned when it is best to shut up and run. Some men learn slower than others and thus they get beat up more than their neighbor. All in all, time will heal the anger, after all both of them know that no one else would put up with either of them if they split, so they hang in there and keep lots of ban-aids.

MULES AND WISDOM

City folks envision us as working at picking corn in a 40-acre field by hand. We do have farm implements; all is not slave (husband) labor. If we don't have what we need to get the work done, we have a neighbor somewhere that will lend us the right tool and maybe come help us plant or gather. That is just cooperation between neighbors, who most likely is kinfolks anyway.

If I have a mule and you have a plow, well, together we will get the work on both our places done and maybe help the other neighbors if they need it. Back in the big city, most people don't know who their neighbor is. Many here still use a mule for the hard work and sometimes the mule is better company than the woman back at the house and in a few cases, prettier too.

Mules do not need gas but sometimes let off a bit while working. You don't have to change the oil in a mule and you can use the byproduct from him. Mules are not stupid. Many a mule is smarter than the person walking behind him holding the plow. Sometimes the mule is better looking than the woman that the farmer is married too also. Stupid is those who won't learn. Ignorant is those who have not been taught.

EQUAL PROFESSIONS

The problem with the outside world is that we here in Coldbeans are seen as uneducated hicks. Well that is true but education it not the measure to use. Many people have graduated from college and never got above level one in the work force. It is not education that counts; it is intelligence and how you apply what you know with what you do. All your education would not help you to plow a straight row or know when to plant and what to plant. Likewise, we would be lost in the big city.

We, all of us, try to work at what we like and we can do best to raise our family. Farming does that for us. It is hard work but rewarding. It does not have the big money that you might get in your work, but it pleases us. The strange thing is that a city fellow will work hard his entire career so that he can retire and get a small place in the country. I don't know of any farmer that wanted to retire and move to the city.

PRIORITIES

Our priorities in life are set by the age we are. As seniors, we want a good retirement income, good health insurance and a place we know where we will be buried. We also hope to still have our own teeth. As a mature adult, we want to be in a profession that will someday reward us with retirements and also provide health insurance. We hope for a loving companion and a nice home with good kids and a sports car and of course a boat for fishing.

As a teen, the priorities are completely different. Their priorities are called "necessities of life to exist". They MUST have a cell phone, an IPOD and money so they can be one of the gang. They want to choose their own clothes and us to have to pay for them.

They wish to have the right to not have to talk to stupid adults who are from the dark ages and know nothing of life or what is important to a teen. If as an adult you think buying a house is the big investment and you hope some day to have it paid for,...well just try to raise a teen. Teens are expensive and teens can not be understood even though they carry your genes. They are as alien as a creature from outer space. I honestly believe that it is easier for our guvmint to run this big country than it is for a parent to raise a teen without having to resort to (a) Drinking, (b) taking dope or (c) checking into a mental hospital for 6 months. The good part of all of this is when the teen grows up and get married and you can observe quietly what he or she will be going thru in a few years. Payback is hell.

SMALL TOWN AMERICA

You can't judge the world by looking out of your window. Likewise, you can't understand us without visiting our little town. The same holds true for us understanding YOU. It is harder for us to get to the big city, lots here rely on the horse and buggy for transportation and we don't think that would be too good in big city traffic. Different people have different lifestyles and we chose the one that best fits our taste. If you enjoy living on the 10th floor of a high-rise apartment bldg, that is good for you but we don't think we would not like it.

We live in homes that you might not find to be so comfortable. We don't have a lot of luxuries, as electricity, running water and heat. We like having to go to the well for water. We like oil lamps (no electric bill to pay) and that is nice because we don't have much cash to pay bills. We live on a lot less income than you do, but we enjoy our lives and we think you enjoy yours. If you don't enjoy it, then think about a change.

We do the most that we can with what we have to do it with. That is true for most people, the rich don't have to worry about survival but most of us do. Be you poor or rich, if you visit us, you will be treated the same way. We welcome guests and enjoy the visit, but we also enjoy when the guest leave. I guess, we are just a normal small town American Community and we like it that way.

INVITE TO POLITICIANS

We, here in Coldbeans think that America is great but like any family, there are things that not everyone agrees with. One thing for sure, is that we here all agree that America is the finest county in the world. That might be because we were born here and live here, but we don't think that is all there is to it. Small towns have a lot of freedom and no one messes with us. We have the right to live our lives without guvmint influence. We do not ask anything of our guvmint but that they spend our money a bit more carefully.

We expect the same thing from our federal guvmint that we do from our local guvmint, they will steal but hopefully not a lot and they will be crooked or else they would be trying some honest type of labor. But, let us be honest about our dishonest politicians. They are the best that money can buy. We have not had a lynching of a politician to my knowledge but having one might make the others think a bit before playing with the money which really is our money, not theirs. Run the country like you run the family if you were poor like us, do without some things, like big limo's and fancy dinners and big apartments. The best way to represent the people is to know the people. From the looks of things, I don't think the guvmint knows us very well. Hey fellows, come on down and visit the taxpayers and see how we live. I think you are afraid of visiting because while you are gone, your compatriots in crime will steal everything that you stole from us.

GOING TO CHURCH

We men all agree that two things are bad about having to go to church on Sunday, First is having to take a bath and the other one is once you are in church you have to stay awake or at least not snore. I can't fake the bath but as long as I don't snore, I can fake the being awake. I like the preachers that just drone along in the same tone all the time. The ones that jump and shout keep me awake. If I have to stay awake through the whole service I am cranky and don't put money in the basket where it is passed. If I am hung over bad, I can fake being awake by sleeping with my eyes open. Yes it can be done with enough practice and a lot of whiskey.

Going to church drunk or hung over is not a nice thing according to the women. We agree but sometimes being drunk makes the sermon go down a bit better, assuming that we even listen. The purpose of church is not to make you a better man, it is to keep the wife happy and thus, you will be happy also. Another reason is if no church, then no Sunday eats. That is the biggest reason for going. It sure ain't going to keep me from that place down under my wife is always telling me I am going there for sure.

PREPARE FOR THE KIDS

Coming back home to where you grew up is a refreshing lift to ones spirits. Wakening up in the same bed you slept in as a child takes you back to those great days when all you had to do was explore and learn about the world around you. There was so much to learn and so many things to do that one wonder how we got all those things done in one childhood.

I think childhood is the greatest of memories. Our mind is selective and wants to remember the best parts of the past. Growing up is not all as we remember it to be. It is colored by time and what we wish to remember the most. Going back home is like a time machine. It triggers many memories that may have been buried for a very long time. Being an adult, we have to think daily of earning a living, taking care of family and all the things adults have to do. As a kid, every moment was new and different. Life was ideal then. But this is reality and we are grown and have responsibilities as parents now, and one of those responsibilities is to teach the children of today how things were when we were young. To kids, the world started with them and all before was not important. Our kids will make mistakes, that is the learning process but the more they know about what WE learned as kids the less likely for them to make the same ones or to recognize them when they do make them.

We can visit the past in our memories and through or children but kids cannot see the future. We must be there to help. For them to have a future, we as parents must do our part now. We cannot give them a guarantee of a good life but we can prepare then to cope with the bad and hope they are lucky like we were at their age to have wise parents to guide them

MAKE IT BETTER

There is an old adage that to the goose, "every day is a new world" and so to should it be for us. Each day is another chance to do sometime positive for someone. Before we were born people cared enough to give us what we have today. We must do the same and leave a better world for someone else. I hope we can do a bit better than some of our predecessors. We can try to give a little less violence, a bit less pollution and a better world than we came into. Animals can only remember from when they started life, humans have the advantage of knowing there was a past and of having hopes for a future for their children. Create things, don't be a destroyer of things. Contribute to the world from what you have to give. One grain of sand does not make a beach but a lot of sand together makes a beach for play and fun to run and dig in. The world is here for US, let us be there for the world. We can hope for no more then to have the future remember us as the ones that left a better world than we found it.

INSECT STUDY

Clemson University is doing a study of Coldbeans residents. The bovine division of Clemson has this idea that since the cave man did not bath, there might be a chance that not bathing could be good protection from insects. They are here to study the life of Caleb, our famous stinker, the one who never gets near water, except when it is brewed into beer. Now in truth, insects are attracted to Caleb but they do not seem to bother him. Really, not much of anything bothers him but the feel of water. Oh well, it gives the town something to watch and laugh at. It also funnels a bit of money into the town. There seems to be something to this theory. Not taking a bath builds up a protective layer that prevents bugs from getting to the skin and thus biting you. They have also found that bugs and insects will stay away from your eyes and nose if you don't wear shoes. The smell seems to attract them to your feet where they go to bite you and then they get sick and die.

The University wants to gather this essence and bottle it as a way to keep the bugs away product but the problem is that it keeps people away also so it might not be beneficial to the general public but might have some use in the military. There might be a problem even with that idea. The Geneva Convention prohibits cruel and unusual punishment but for some reason do not outlaw bombs and guns from warfare. Go figure that logic. There is also the "cruelty to insects society" trying to stop this experiment.

FAMILY IDIOTS

"Keeping it in the family" usually means family secrets but sometimes it pertains to marriages. Marrying kin is not restricted to the south but seems to be the joke for stupid southerners.

Very few marriages are within the same family but sometime it happens. Most of those times the kinship was not known to all in the family before the marriage until someone admits being familiar with the other side more than normally.

If it is cousins that marry that is not to bad but the closer the kin the more the worry that any children will be idiots. Don't think we hate idiots; some of the finest people in Coldbeans are idiots. Being stupid is not the problem, being stupid and kin is. Once they are married and the baby is on the way it is too late to stop the future family. The only hope is that people will not notice or comment on the close similarity of the kid to both sides of the family. Another hope is that the idiot might grow up and go into politics.

RELIGION

Everyone wants to believe in heaven and that they are doing the right thing to get there. What if you went to the pearly gates and St Peter said, sorry, only the Catholics are allowed, you are Baptist and can't come in. What if it was reversed and you got in and your friend who was Catholic could not cause it was only for Baptist? See how stupid this difference in religion is. So, if we all can get to heaven, why are there so many religions? The answer might make you mad but humans invented religion way back in the cave man days. He was frightened of the world and found something to help him be not afraid. He worshiped the sun or the moon or a certain star. So what can you believe? It does not matter or it is very lonely up there because a lot of people are wrong.

You will be surprised if you get to heaven and you see a lot of people that you knew would never get there. Believe what you wish, and allow others the same freedom. One of you might be wrong and no one knows which one it is.

LET THE KID OUT

What is the best age to be adult-Child-Retired-Very old, and the answer is—the age that you are now. In truth, we want to be a child again, but with the wisdom we now have but that is having your cake and eating it too. The best age to be is the age before when you are told not to do it and the age that it is fun to do and people think it is cute. It is all right to fall if you are small and it does not hurt your butt. It is cute to get food all over you when you are a baby learning new things. It is fun to see the wonders of the world thru fresh eyes. As adults we do not do these things and sometimes we want to but we are now trained to act like an adult and inside of us the child is saying, "I don't want to be grow up right now."

We may be adults and have to act as adults but we can be kids by observing life thru the actions of the kids. We can say to our selves that we wish we could be down there doing the same thing, but alas, we are adults and adults are not supposed to behave like that. We can sing in the shower or play with the soap in the tub, IF no one is around to see or hear us. The sad thing is that we are afraid to do the things that others also want to do but they are also afraid to do them. It is sad to lose the child inside of us.

THE MOON

On a cold night, with clear skies and no clouds, you can look up at the moon and wonder, "men walked on that thing a long time ago". At that time it seemed to be a new beginning for the world, a world united as one great blue globe and venturing into space. But we had more important things to do here, like kill a lot of people, fight with each other and become distrustful of our neighbors.

The moon is still there, unharmed by man. If he went there, it would have beer cans and campaign banners all over the place, one side would belong to some people and they would want to control the other side, which belong to other people. It might be best to stay home, so we don't make other worlds as bad as this one. It was a better world when animals ate each other. That was for food, but now we kill because someone does not think like we do. Moon, if you are smart, you will keep man away. This was thunk up by a country boy with no education but a lot of people smarts.

WHEN TO BATHE

Bathing is important to the women, but men seem to be a bit more indifferent to it. In fact, if it were not for the women, men would not bathe at all or at least only when the flies get bad.

Bathing is required if you are going to church on Sunday. It is also good to bathe on Saturday if you are going out drinking with the boys, and carousing for women. If you take a bath on Saturday night then you should not be required to take one on Sunday morning if you are hung over. That could at times get you out of going to church. You may find this strange but bathing is a big chore, first you have to bring in the water and heat it, and put the man in the tub but the hard part is getting the men to cooperate and use SOAP. Soap is not harmful but some soap makes you smell funny and the other men might think you smell a bit like a woman. Social mores are very strange and complicated here in Coldbeans.

THE WIVES

There are two supper times in Coldbeans, one is when the wife decides to cook supper and the other is when the husband comes home from work. If the husband prefers to drink and run around and not work, then he might find himself going a bit hungry or eating some very nasty meals prepared by a very mean wife. It is true that we have a sheriff here but the wife of the house enforces the laws better than the law enforcement of Coldbeans ever could.

I guess all over the world, women do the rules. If men wanted rules they would be a bit different. There would be more thou shall and a lot less thou shalts nots. Sometimes we men would love to kill he wife but deep inside where no one can see, we know that without her, our life would be a lot worse. A wise man settles for the least worse thing and tries to adapt to it.

Women do the raising of the kids, she teaches the girls that men are lazy louts and not worth killing and she teaches the boys that they will be next to nothing when they grow up and most times she is right. We men are born with a reputation and we do not have to do anything to earn it, only be born a male is enough. The strange thing is that the worse we are treated, the more we chase women and we are looking for women that are not a bit like our mothers.

When we decide to get hitched (we don't really do the deciding) we pick a woman just like mom. Men are taught from early childhood that we are bad and always should be treated as such. That explains why most of the wives here are mean as a run over snake.

THE BARBER FAMILY

For all of the strange goings on in Coldbeans and the weird families that live here there is one that stands out. The Barbers have lived here for a long time and the guvmint came around and asked question about them We here are a bit closed mouth when it comes to the guvmint asking questions.
We said, the Barbers were a nice family and well known and well liked in the community. We also volunteered that to our knowledge, the Barber's ain't shot or killed anyone and the only time one of them was in jail was for public drunk and that ain't really no crime here about. It seems that for the last 5 generations, the Barbers ain't buried any family members according to guvmint records and they are still getting the checks but the checks ain't been cashed for years. This raised a bit of questions in the Social Security office and made their computers a bit off.

A couple of us went with the guvmint officials to visit the barber's and we were greeted nice and friendly like. We were even asked to sit a spell and have some tea or maybe a bit of the homemade stuff. We accepted but the guvmint workers declined. After a howdy and all the names were said, we got down to the business we all came out about. The explanation was so simple that it could have been handled over the phone but the guvmint does things the hard way. The reason that the barber's were still getting those checks was that no one had notified the guvmint about anyone dying in the family. The daddy, the granddaddy and two uncles had died and their check was a still coming. Naturally, the guvmint don't trust peoples word and wanted proof so the family took them out to the family plot on the back of the land and showed them the graves. Well that explained the kin being dead but why were they still getting checks and no one had told the guvmint about it? "Well sir" said the head barber, "we don't trouble you and if'n you wanted to keep sending the money that was your business" The officials were about to burst and wanted the whole family arrested. Some one had to step in and show some common sense and there are not a lot of people around here qualified to do that, so I did.

The senior Mr. Barber went to the back room and got all the checks, still in their envelopes and gave them to the guvmint official. This action kind of took the wind out of the guvmint guy's sail but there was nothing that he could think of to cover the event as it was a first to them. There ain't no law in being stupid and the case was closed and the matter forgotten. Alls well that ends well I say.

THE GRAVEYARD

For the first time that I can remember, it is time to enlarge the graveyard. We don't burry a lot of people here, most go on family plots on family land and so the cemetery don't get a lot of business. The task is not hard, all we have to do is move the fence a bit so we can get more in there. The land was given to the city a long time ago, we just have been too lazy (meaning can't find sober people to work) and so the task just ain't got done. A few people here are a bit strange about walking on ground where people is buried. They still believe in haunts and ghost. Of course drinking helps some of them to be a bit braver and drink also helps some of them to be more frightened. We have a rule, no alcohol in the graveyard. If you can't share, don't drink. I think some of the people buried here would be willing to drink too after so long without a good drink. But to be sure, no alcohol allowed in the graveyard. The men work hard, clearing the ground and getting it mowed and nice looking. It almost makes you want to die just to be buried here. The women cook and have ice tea, but most of us brought our own drinks. Some day we got to teach the women about corn likker.

It was a one-day task and all was glad when it was done and all thought it was quite pretty. One couple wanted to move their house here and set up home but we vetoed that idea quick and the bad thing is they were sober when they made the suggestion.

LOGIC?

It may sound stupid but sometimes if you have a very complicated problem to solve, don't go to the bright guy for the answer. Ask a stupid person as in us hicks in the country. Many problems that you city folks have we here think are easy to solve. You see, the smarter you are the more levels you think on the more options you have for any problem. Problems are solved by only one answer and to have many possible ones and all are reasonable only further complicates the question. We country folks think on a straight line, there is a problem so how do we fix it? Intelligent people think of how the solution will affect people, environment, living conditions. jobs and money etc.

How many medications have we put out for people to trust and use and then later on find they are harmful to some few people that are blue eyed and left handed so they are pulled from the market? If that medicine helps thousand obtain relief and only 5 died then which is the greater good? Should all suffer for so few that had something else wrong that caused them to react?

It is which end of the telescope you are looking thru; if I put up a fence it is to keep my animals IN, not to keep people out. Cars kill (or drivers do) but does that mean that we should all stop driving? We need a pill called common sense and we should give it to the politicians for free and make sure they take them. All new things are risks. Every day we wake up could be our last. So the government should tell us not to get up? Not to do normal things? We could be harmed. Bah Humbug!

COLDBEANS COURT HOUSE

Our court house, or city hall or whatever you want to call it is not very big. We only have three workers plus the mayor and his secretary/mistress. There is not a lot of paper keeping to do which is good if you are a guvmint worker since filing is work and work is not part of a guvmint workers job. One of the "clerks" is the greeter; it is her job to find out what you are doing there and are you looking for information or spying on t the workers? The second girl is the blocker. It is her job to find a way to prevent you from finding someone that knows what you want or preventing you from finding the place to find the information you are looking for. The third girl is the supervisor; every office of two or more workers must have a supervisor. It is her job to not help you. That is the job of the people that work for her. If the federal Guvmint wants to keep national security information from the enemy, here is the place to store it. Nothing gets out of there that is useful or needed. The gold at Fort Knox is not as well protected as documents at city hall.

We are proud of our city hall workers. They excel in doing very little and work very hard at it. They are devoted to their mission that nothing useful is ever given out. If we could only get Washington to be this efficient!

A GOOD HONEST CROOK

Somewhere south of us is the upper crust city of CHARLESton, as they pronounce it and look down their noses as they say it. To the NAWTH of us is the capital city of sin or Columbia as they want to be called. Most people there are nice but they have the chore of putting up with all the state politicians and that hurts their image. Smack in-between is our lovely little town of Coldbeans, where you know your neighbor and your politician and which one to trust. Now, we are not perfect but our claim to fame is we are too stupid to be dishonest so we can be trusted.

It is not that we don't trust our politicians; we expect them to be crooked, which is why we elect them. It would be useless to send an honest man to Columbia and we certainly would not send a good honest man to Washington. If we vote in a politician we want him to be as efficient as the other crooks. We keep the stupid crooks here as mayor and sheriff. That way they can steal from each other and leave us alone. If more people followed our example, they would not be so disappointed with their elected officials. If you know they are gonna be crooked, at least get a good crook, not one so stupid as to get caught. If they are really good at being crooked, they could go to Washington and maybe some day even the white house,

SKUNKS GIRLFRIEND

If you been reading carefully and remember Skunk Caleb and his smell then you know he is a lonely man and there is no hope here in Coldbeans for a companion for him. There might be a ray of hope though; I got a letter from a lady that reads this paper and lives in upstate SC. She wants to meet Skunk and see if they get along. Now I wrote back and told her about his "little" problem. Frankly, that he stinks. She explained that the smell would not bother her as when she was running with a motorcycle gang and she fell off the back of the cycle and her nose was completely ripped off and she can't smell at all now. This might work out for the both of them. Skunk is a bit untrained in female company and she might have her hands full with him but he can be trained to do everything but bathing. The lady has no male friends because of her face but seems nice and sincere. Skunk went to the general store and bought a few nice clothes to wear and if you are wondering how he did that? It was by going to the back window and telling them what he wanted and they tossed the stuff out to him like they do his annual bar of soap. He is excited to finally meet a woman who will not run from him and she is hoping that the two of them get along.
We wish them good luck.

PROTECTING THE CAPITAL

As the saying goes "out of the mouths of babes or sometimes fools and there is logic in stupid ideas. Harvey Muckenfuss made a brilliant suggestion to this paper and I pass it on to the Politicians to ponder. We can make the Capital building in Washington terrorist proof and at the same time exhibit our freedom of political information to the public. The idea is so simple that it took a simple mind to think of it.

We attach loud speakers to all sides of the Capital and play what is happening on the floor of the senate or the house live to the people standing around and watching or taking pictures. Anyone lingering more than 3 minutes has to have a sinister purpose and is not a true American. Therefore he must be up to no good and should be arrested. This idea could be carried even further and it could be used for rehabilitation of inmates. We could pipe Congress live and loud to all the prisons in the country. Once hearing of this, people will be discouraged from crime or only commit crime on an elected official. I guess the ACLU would consider this action to be cruel and inhuman punishment. Dang, sometimes we country hicks amaze even us with our logic.

WISDOM OF SENILITY

The nice thing about being old and forgetful or in the eyes of the young is being "senile" is that time that we can remember nice things but we forget the bad things. Being from a country town, we have a lot less bad to forget and a lot more of good to remember. Another nice thing about being old and senile is that if we are lonely, we can talk to ourselves and be in perfect agreement with what we say. Sure, we can't remember birthdays and also at times, some of the kid's names, but we do remember the wonderful times spent with who ever you are.

TESTIMONIALS ABOUT COLDBEANS

I want to thank all the wonderful people that wrote me about my little book, I did it for people to enjoy stories from the South; here are some of the comments

JOE CLAPJAW, Poboy Ga.
I sore did liak yo little book. My daughter reed it to me and I laughed so hard I spit up my possum stew

TOM BERRY, age 9
My daddy red some of youse book to me and he thought it was funny, but then he also drools all the time.

MARY PETERS, Pebble Ark
I bought your book; it is just the right size to fit under the short leg on the table in the bathroom.

LOU ELLEN SQUAT somewhere in NY
My mother bought your book for me; she said it is so that I will study hard in school and not live in Coldbeans

LOUIE, THE PUSHER, Homeboy
Hey I lake yo book man, When I am high it makes a lot of sense

INMATE 2397826345 SC state prison system Hey man real groovy, now I wish I had bought the book instead of stealing it. I am in the infirmary here with a knife wound from the guy that did buy it and did not want to read it.

People are more forgiving of old and senile people but we can still serve a good purpose in life. I think it would be a good idea to send us to Washington. We might even get a better congress than we are paying for now. You all have a nice day, you hear!